IT WAS THRILLING AND FORBIDDEN—

this stolen rendezvous in the very heart of the bayous, and Kate somehow felt she would never be the same again.

Hal's face was in shadow, but she felt his eyes upon her as his hand slipped around her shoulders to draw her close. His head moved over hers, blocking the stars, and his lips found hers, nuzzling and exploring.

"I can't stop touching you," he whispered, caressing her tenderly. "I want you so much," he said, beginning to undo the buttons of her blouse.

And in that moment, she desperately wanted him too. Her desire was like a waterfall inside her, tumbling and roaring, sweeping away all thought of tomorrow, all thought of anything but her longing and her love . . .

ESTELLE EDWARDS, a nationally known author, wrote her first play at ten and her first novel at twenty. She grew up in the West, and after a brief stint as an actress in New York City, she settled in Hollywood, where she writes books and films and indulges her interests in American jazz, antique cars, and romance. She is the author of another Rapture Romance, *Moonslide*.

Dear Reader:

The editors of Rapture Romance have only one thing to say—thank you! Your response to our authors, both the newcomers and the established favorites, has been enthusiastic and loyal, and we, who love our books, appreciate it.

We are committed to bringing you romances after your own heart, with the tender sensuality you've asked for and the quality you deserve. We hope that you will continue to enjoy all six Rapture Romances each month as much as we enjoy bringing them to you.

To tell you about upcoming books, introduce you to the authors, and give you an inside look at the world of Rapture Romance, we have started a free monthly newsletter. Just write to *The Rapture Reader* at the address shown below, and we will be happy to send you each issue.

And please keep writing to us! Your comments and letters have already helped us to bring you better and better books—the kind *you* want—and we depend on them. Of course, our authors also eagerly await your letters. While we can't give out their addresses, we are happy to forward any mail—writers need to hear from their fans!

Happy reading!

Robin Grunder, Editor
Rapture Romance
New American Library
1633 Broadway
New York, NY 10019

THE KNAVE OF HEARTS

by

Estelle Edwards

RAPTURE ROMANCE

NEW AMERICAN LIBRARY

NAL BOOKS ARE AVAILABLE AT QUANTITY DISCOUNTS
WHEN USED TO PROMOTE PRODUCTS OR SERVICES.
FOR INFORMATION PLEASE WRITE TO PREMIUM MARKETING DIVISION,
THE NEW AMERICAN LIBRARY, INC., 1633 BROADWAY,
NEW YORK, NEW YORK 10019.

SIGNET, SIGNET CLASSIC, MENTOR, PLUME, MERIDIAN AND NAL BOOKS
are published by The New American Library, Inc.,
1633 Broadway, New York, New York 10019

First Printing, January, 1984

1 2 3 4 5 6 7 8 9

PRINTED IN THE UNITED STATES OF AMERICA

Chapter One

❧

"You sure do sound hot about it, miss." The deep voice of the man on the telephone rumbled with energy and humor.

"*Ms.* Sewell," she replied briskly, "and I am at this very moment standing in a New Orleans hotel lobby where there is no record of my reservation, Mr. Lewis. I find that incredible."

The man was clearly inept. She wondered that the steamboat line would employ him to deal with the public. Much more of his casual attitude and she would become really irritated.

"Our line is very popular," he said teasingly. He seemed to be convinced she was trying to book passage without a reservation. "It's booked months in advance, and you just can't—"

"Mr. Lewis," she interrupted, speaking distinctly but without rancor as she flipped a lock of her sandy hair away from her face. "I don't think you've been listening to me. If you check your files, I know you will find the reservation from my travel agent in San Francisco, and when you do, I would appreciate your calling this hotel immediately so I can stay here—in a room, not in the lobby. This hotel, they

5

tell me, is completely booked, so I'm just going to sit down until you call back."

Laughing, he agreed to check the files, but the tone of his voice had an edge of doubt in it. Kate replaced the receiver. The assistant manager stared at her from behind the barricade of the front desk.

"He doesn't believe me," Kate said. The manager shrugged.

Irritated, angry, but still feeling a tickle of humor in the face of all arrangements gone awry, Kate sat down in a wicker chair. Where was her long-anticipated vacation now? She sighed, then smiled wryly.

Leaning back for a moment, she closed her brown eyes. Yes, it would all work out—just as her career had. She had worked her way through college and law school, always finding some job that would fit around her schedule, and had passed the bar exam a scant few months after graduation. She had gone into public-service law with all the energy of someone who wanted to make a difference.

As she thought about her practice, watching people mill about the high-ceilinged Victorian hotel, she noticed a tall, lean, red-haired man come through the swinging doors. He had buoyant good looks and a sexy walk, moving slowly and easily, with confidence and just the trace of a swagger. He stopped at the front desk.

Now there's a man, she thought as she saw him lean against the counter and motion to the assistant manager. An easy smile warmed his face as he talked to the man, who, at that moment, raised his head slightly and nodded—at her. Kate rose, perplexed; the red-haired man turned to face her. The ready smile widened, and even at that distance she saw his eyes light with pleasure. He cast himself off from the desk with a graceful movement and stood erect, waiting for her to reach him. He had a sultry, sensual quality that invaded her senses as she approached. This man wouldn't rush to a phone or run for a cab; he would take his time, savoring experiences large and small.

"Miss Sewell, this is Mr. Lewis from the riverboat line," said the assistant manager.

Kate was astonished. The pleasure she'd felt while watching the man move across the lobby evaporated. Was *this* person the rude oaf on the telephone?

"Your reservation has been located," the man said quietly. "Everything is in order now." He smiled slowly.

"I'm glad to hear that," she replied, still trying to match *this* man with the unpleasant image she had formed from the telephone conversation. But it was, undoubtedly, the same rich voice.

"I am, too, and you have all my apologies." He had a way of fastening his soft, knowledgeable eyes on her face—eyes that seemed to probe gently and deeply. She did not feel unclothed as much as she felt revealed by his look. One would not keep secrets from such a man; his eyes seemed to say that he already knew them and understood.

"I'll have your bags sent up, Miss Sewell," the assistant manager was saying loudly, as though repeating something she hadn't heard. He rang a bell.

Turning away from the desk and away from the assistant manager, Lewis said, "My company would like to invite you for dinner and cocktails." His voice was purring; his eyes did not leave her face. "It's the least we can do."

Kate was starving but nothing on earth would have allowed her to dine with him. Typical man, she thought. Thinks he can make up for anything with a little charm and a meal. She declined his offer politely.

"Oh, but I insist," he said, taking her arm.

"Really, Mr. Lewis, it isn't necessary."

"Hal."

"I'm not in the least bit hungry. All I want is a hot bath and a little peace." All she wanted to do was flee.

"The bar is this way," he said softly and persuasively. "You'll like it, and it will give me a chance to apologize again and again." He smiled down at her, and she couldn't help laughing. He really was trying to be nice, and she was acting like a real stick.

"All right," she said. "You've convinced me." Taking his arm, she followed him.

The bar was hung in sweltering red velvet, its table area caged off in elaborately wrought iron, reminiscent of nineteenth-century New Orleans.

When they were seated, Lewis began to apologize again, but she waved it away. "I see you're tired of apologies," he said, still smiling. His lips curled upward at the edges, sweeping in to a full center.

"I should be apologizing to you now," she said. "But you *were* a bear on the telephone."

"I was only teasing, to make you loosen up a bit. You sounded so . . . brittle. But you have a beautiful voice—clear, not loud. I bet people listen to you."

Hum, she thought, transparent flattery. She said, "They usually do." She glanced up at him. "Were you putting me on about the reservation being lost?"

"No. It wasn't filed with the hotel, that's all. A mix-up." He smiled roguishly, examining her face with his dark brown eyes. His glance had no shyness in it but, rather, established an instant, probing intimacy. She turned away to break the spell. The waiter arrived and they ordered.

"You aren't the sort of traveler we usually get," he said when the waiter had left.

"What sort is that?" Kate asked.

"You're traveling alone. That's number one. Or"— he looked up—"are you joining someone on board?"

Kate looked at him, not knowing how she wanted to answer his question. He had annoyed her, then placated her, and now she found he fascinated her. It was clearly time to put him in his place.

"I'm an attorney with a firm in San Francisco, and I'm on my first vacation," she said in her most serious tone.

"That's *two*," he exclaimed triumphantly.

"What is?" she asked, puzzled.

"First, you're traveling alone, and now you tell me you're an attorney. You really are unusual. What kind of law do you practice?"

"Public law," she said lightly. He looked at her quizzically, long dark lashes sweeping across a few freckles around his questioning eyes. But, gazing at him, Kate didn't feel like describing the invigorating, underfunded, uphill battles for environmental protection, tenants' rights, and discrimination in employment that made up her practice.

He broke the silence. "How long have you been an attorney?" he asked.

"Five years now."

"And no vacation?" He sounded scolding.

Kate changed the subject. "I'm also an American-history buff, and I've always wanted to see the Mississippi River."

He said nothing. She pushed her sandy, bobbed hair back from her face, a little uncomfortable under his unbroken and admiring gaze. Her long fingers, tipped with pale pink nails, curled around the stem of her wineglass.

"This is just the trip to take," he finally said energetically. "Lots of American history and lots of Mississippi."

"How long have you worked for the boat line?" Kate asked.

"About three years." He tossed off the words. "Look, I know you're angry about my teasing on the phone and I'm very sorry. It was just . . . oh, never mind. Can we be friends?" he finished disarmingly.

She felt the smile start before it widened on her face. "Yes, of course," she said. She liked his directness. "I'm a little on edge, I guess. The plane was terribly delayed, one of my bags has been lost—though I suppose they'll find it when we're near Natchez or someplace—and I just lost a big case that I really wanted to win."

Hal Lewis raised an eyebrow. "Sounds like you need this vacation. At least you have something to look forward to." He began to talk about the journey ahead, the stops at Vicksburg and Oak Alley, and the life on board the boat.

"It's called a boat, you know, not a ship."

"And it's called a stateroom, not a cabin," she added.

He laughed. "Aha. You *have* done this before, after all."

"No. I did some reading. But I'm afraid most of

what I know about steamboats was written in the nineteenth century, when people like Mrs. Trollope and Mark Twain were cruising up and down the Mississippi."

"You'll find this boat a great deal grander than the ones they rode. Since you're a history buff, you'll like the history lectures. And there are movies and a gym and a sauna. There's a party for singles one night and dancing every night. Most people just eat and drink their way through it all. The lounge is fun—it's at the tail end of the observation deck."

All this was delivered in a gentle monotone, his eyes never leaving her face, but somehow it wasn't in the least boring. He reached out and touched her hand with his fingertips. "Too bad I can't go with you—yes?"

Too much, too soon, she thought even as she realized she found the idea enticing. She rose. "Thank you very much for the drink, the preview, and the apology."

"Must you go?" he asked quietly as he, too, rose.

"Afraid so." She smiled. He made her uneasy, for he provoked feelings in her that she'd kept under wraps for a long time.

"No dinner?"

"Not tonight, thanks. Perhaps some other time."

"I trust so, though I can't imagine how," he said, and even though they only shook hands, it was not her imagination that his touch was more like a caress than a simple farewell.

With a scream from the whistle, the boat pulled away. Shaped rather like a big white wedding cake—flat on the bottom and built in tiers straight up to the swimming pool on the sun deck—the huge riverboat churned into the harbor. The cruise was to last seven days, moving upriver from New Orleans to St. Louis, straight through America's historical Southland. Kate leaned on the rail and felt the anticipation rising within her as she looked out at a fairyland of glimmering lights—the New Orleans harbor. The boat's immense calliope played deafening renditions of "Bill Bailey" and "Oh, Susannah," and Kate could feel each note reverberating in every bone of her body. People milled around the dock, stirred by the beat of the music and hundreds of passengers leaned over the railing on either side of Kate, waving, laughing, and yelling.

Jostled by the exuberant passengers who tried in vain to yell over the boom and shriek of the calliope, Kate turned away from thoughts of her work and threw herself into the general hilarity. One woman at the railing was pouring champagne into paper cups and passing them around; a man next to her, whooping a rebel yell, boated his hat out across the harbor.

It was hard not to be infected by the jollity around her, but her thoughts kept turning back to the night before and to the man with bronze hair—Hal Lewis. The memory of him, even now, irritated her but it made her tingle, too.

What utter nonsense, she said to herself, and resolutely turned her attention back to the fading, blinking light of New Orleans. But the memory of Hal Lewis would not be pushed aside.

The boat plowed north. She shook off her trailing thoughts and left the rail for her stateroom.

Pleasantly surprised by its size, she wondered for

one mad moment if Hal had had anything to do with its selection. It was painted a warm, bright yellow, and its two windows and an outside door opened to a veranda overlooking the river. A small white table and chairs outside promised leisurely hours of coffee or cocktails. Ah, she thought, this is a vacation.

She dressed for dinner slowly, savoring her new setting. Her stateroom was just below the observation deck and just above the deck where the officers' quarters, the forward lounge, and the purser's office were located. Kate walked up to the Grand Salon, the dining room, passing the almost deserted gift shop and a little bar from which raucous music and voices came.

The salon was huge, full of white-draped tables, bustling waiters, and an extraordinary array of buffet food. The maître d', a tall man who resembled nothing so much as a stork, rose up before her, greeting her with professional warmth. He checked his list, then grinned.

"An excellent choice, Miss Sewell. You'll enjoy this table."

"You say that to everyone, I bet," she replied, laughing.

"That's true," he suddenly admitted, leading her across the room, "but I meant it this time." He stopped at an exuberantly festive table. Kate relished the moment, looking at the four people with whom she would dine for the next seven days, people she'd never met before and probably would never see after the trip. "I would like to introduce Miss Kate Sewell," the maître d' said.

A tall, burly black-haired man of about thirty-five took charge. He offered her a chair opposite him, having first quickly glanced to make sure there were none nearer to him.

"Please," he said, "then we'll make all the introductions."

His name, it turned out, was Roland Dupuis. He had high, peaked brows arched over dark brown eyes. A short mustache and a cleft in his chin completed him.

"Allow me to present my sister, Cynthia," he said in an aggressively courtly manner.

"How do you do," Cynthia said in a high, breathless voice. She was as fair as he was dark. Though she seemed beautiful in a fragile way, her pale eyes gleamed sharply behind her fashionable glasses.

"And this is Mrs. Pike," Roland went on, turning toward a woman of about sixty. Small and pert, she virtually twinkled at Kate.

"Nancy Lee," she said warmly. "How are you? Been round the boat yet?"

"No, not really, but I'm looking forward to exploring it," Kate said, liking the older woman immediately.

"And next to Mrs. Pike, Matthew Hitchins," said Dupuis, sitting down. Hitchins was also about sixty, an athletically built man, lean, hard, and weathered. He wore expensive but conservative clothes.

"Mr. Hitchins was just telling us about his real estate business in St. Louis," Dupuis was saying.

"Everyone calls me Hitch," he said. He had hazel eyes and creases in his cheeks.

"Please call me Kate. Are you in business, too?" she asked Mrs. Pike.

"Retired. College professor." She had lots of curly gray hair and almost black eyes. "American history."

"Oh, one of my favorite subjects," Kate exclaimed.

"I'm in the oil business," interjected Roland, taking the conversation back. "Refinement. Louisiana." His long, narrow eyes regarded her cordially. Suddenly she thought again of Hal Lewis, whose look had been so gentle in its appraisement, as though he knew her inside out and liked her. Roland's look was different—more that of an entrepreneur evaluating a new product.

"My sister is in banking," Roland was saying.

Kate looked at Cynthia. She seemed about thirty, but something about her made her seem much younger. The combination of immaturity and shrewdness was odd, Kate thought.

"And you?" Cynthia asked Kate.

"I'm a lawyer in San Francisco."

After a few minutes of conversation about their respective careers, during which Roland made no effort to hide his attraction to Kate, Nancy Lee shifted the conversation back to the upcoming trip.

"I've been up and down maybe twenty times," Nancy Lee said. "I jes' love it. That old river never lets you down. Neither does the boat. I can't get enough of either of them—I guess you could call me a real river rat." Then, in a different tone, she asked Kate, "How are you going to spend your time on the boat?"

"I'll just be glad to rest by the pool if the weather's good."

Cynthia nudged Kate. "You ought to make friends with the purser. He's pretty good-looking for an older man."

"Would you say he's the best-looking man on this boat?" Nancy Lee teasingly asked Cynthia.

Cynthia smiled prettily. "No. He can't hold a candle to the gambler."

"A real gambler?" asked Kate.

"No, he's an employee of the boat—usually an out-of-work actor from Nashville," Nancy Lee said. "He plays the part of the old-time riverboat gambler— all dolled up in fancy clothes—they were usually pretty good-looking guys." To Cynthia she said, "This one's a real looker, I agree. He's also a fine fellow— lot of class, inside and out." She turned back to Kate. "He plays poker with anyone who wants a friendly hand and sets up the other card games. There's bridge and rummy—"

"Don't sell her on him too hard, Nancy Lee," Cynthia said. "I've had my eye on him and I sure do hope to see him tonight." She rolled her pale blue eyes at Kate and giggled.

Kate listened with half an ear. She could not get the image of Hal Lewis out of her head. She wondered if she would ever see him again, and she was sorry now that she hadn't had dinner with him.

"What's our first stop?" Hitch asked Nancy Lee.

"Oak Alley and the Bon Séjour mansion. Tomorrow afternoon," she answered, smiling at him. "It's one of the most beautiful sites left in the South."

"I would like to show you before then that Southern courtesy is far from dead," Roland said. "Won't you all join me for an after-dinner drink in the lounge?" Roland was looking at Kate with expectation in his eyes. The invitation was well timed; when he directed it at the whole table, she realized it would be ungracious to refuse.

The lounge was spacious and crowded. Flickering lamps cast a warm glow, but what caught Kate's eye immediately was the huge, majestic paddle wheel. It stood two stories high behind the colored-glass windows of the lounge and churned lazily away at the dark Mississippi with a mesmerizing grace.

Roland had just put a hand under her arm and was leading her toward a table through the noisy, convivial room when Kate saw the gambler. His broad shoulders were encased in a dark satin tuxedo, and a frilled shirt stood out at his neck. One leg was crossed casually over the other, and his extraordinary eyes were, in turn, fixed on each person at his table as he dealt out the cards.

"Hal Lewis," Kate breathed.

The deal complete, he put the deck aside, looked up, and saw her.

Chapter Two

❧

"What did you say?" asked Roland, pulling out a chair for her.

"Nothing," Kate answered. She shook her head. The little band was playing vigorously, and it was hard to hear. Hal was still looking at her, but she pretended not to notice. The *gambler*. Why the deception that he had an administrative job? He must have known they would be on the same boat. But these thoughts were soon overwhelmed by her sensations: her heart was beating rapidly and her breath was shallow. Her first instinct was to go up and speak to him, but she held herself back. And what would she say to him? she asked herself. Read him out for fibbing? Say, "Gee whiz, Mr. Lewis, fancy meeting you here"?

"What would you like to drink?" Roland asked her.

"Just white wine, please," she said, shamelessly smiling at him more warmly than she would have if Hal had not been looking at them.

The distance between Kate and Hal was about thirty feet across celebrating tables of passengers. There was a small dance floor to her right, and he was straight ahead in a kind of alcove off the main room. Nancy Lee and Hitch were just sitting down and Cynthia was standing next to her brother, looking at Hal. Finally Cynthia broke her gaze when Hal acknowledged her wave, and she sat down.

It was several moments after Kate was served her wine that she thought she was calm enough to acknowledge Hal herself. She timed the turning of her head and the look of surprise and pleasure on her face, waiting for him to look up. When their eyes met, she shivered deliciously; he looked at her as if she were the only person he'd ever known or ever thought about. She smiled at him, and he raised one eyebrow and nodded. She heard Cynthia say above her, "I see you've caught the glance of the gambler. Isn't he cute?" Kate nodded without shifting her gaze.

Nancy Lee said to Kate, "*That's* Hal. I see he's in fine fettle. Doesn't he look the part?"

"He certainly does," Kate replied. "It's hard to think of him in any other line of work. Does he do this often, or is this a special occasion?"

"Oh, I guess he's been on the boat a couple of years now. People like him. They don't bet real money, you understand—it's just for fun. A free drink or a prize, you know."

"Isn't he something?" Cynthia sighed.

Kate had no idea what she would have said. Luckily, Hitch saved her from having to answer by asking for a dance. Laughing, she agreed, and was swept onto the dance floor. She enjoyed the lively music, even enjoyed knowing Roland was watching her. But she couldn't stop watching Hal, and she couldn't help but notice Cynthia get up and go over to him. Hal ran his hand over his curly red hair and smiled boyishly at Cynthia as she leaned down to whisper something in his ear. He shook his head but offered her a chair at the table, which she accepted with alacrity.

It was after two in the morning. The band had packed up, and though many people had staggered off to their rooms, a dozen determined celebrants remained, playing a slow but enthusiastic game of charades.

Kate turned to go and bumped into Hal Lewis, who had come up behind her.

"Good trip so far?" he asked.

Before she could answer, she heard Nancy Lee call out, "Who's next?"

Kate saw Cynthia rising expectantly from her chair as she heard Hal cry out, "*We'll* do one." He grabbed Kate's wrist and raised her arm above her head. Cynthia sat back and reached for her cigarettes.

"Fine," said Nancy Lee.

"No, no," said Kate, "I can't do this at all."

Cynthia sulked prettily.

"You have five minutes to get your act together," Nancy Lee called cheerily. "Pick a hard one."

She and Hal were no sooner out in the hall, and the door closed, than he put a hand on her arm and turned to face her.

"I want to apologize," he said immediately.

"Again?" She laughed, and he looked sheepishly at his feet.

It's not mysterious or anything, just . . . silly," he said.

"What is?"

"I . . . I thought I was scheduled on the other

boat, leaving a day later, and then at the last minute Chuck got sick and I had to take this one. I tell you, I was sweating it out until you discovered me in my gambler getup."

"You did lead me astray, didn't you? Why?"

He leaned against the pillar and looked down at the floor. "It sounds funny to say, 'How do you do, I'm an actor playing a gambler.' It was the sheerest chance that I was in the office when your call came in. I was talking to this boat's pilot, Andy Tobias. He got me this job. The phone was ringing and ringing, and no one was answering it, so I just picked it up and . . ." His dark eyes swept her face.

"And?"

"And I liked the sound of your voice. So I started to tease you, and the rest is history." His golden eyebrows shot up a little, and he smiled hopefully. "But I can't say I'm sorry it worked out this way— being assigned to your boat—even if I do have to eat humble pie."

"Mr. Lewis, I cannot imagine you ever eating humble pie. But you don't have to apologize—it's not important." But even as she spoke she knew he had become important, and without an explanation from him she could not have felt as good about him as she wanted to. "I mean"—she smiled, feeling her cheeks crinkle—"I mean, I am glad you told me what happened because I was very puzzled."

His hand, at his side until now, reached out gently to curl around hers, holding it wholly within his own, tenderly. He looked at her face, then raised the hand that held hers and brushed his lips against her fingers. Her heart beat more rapidly. How bewildering he was. She saw his face draw close to hers and felt her lips part in anticipation.

"*Hey*. Aren't you ready yet?"

It was Nancy Lee.

"Yes, we are," Kate said rapidly. She looked at him for agreement.

"Then, come in—everyone's waiting. I thought one of you had fallen over the side." Nancy Lee disappeared.

"Heavens, what are we going to do?"

"About what?" he asked carefully.

"About the famous name we're supposed to act out."

Hal shrugged.

"I know—Sea Biscuit," Kate suggested. His head whipped around and he looked at her strangely. But he agreed and they went back into the lounge, to join the spirited competition.

It was near dawn when the game broke up. As Hal walked Kate out onto the deck, she became aware of the silence surrounding the boat, broken only by the clicks and buzzes of the river insects.

"Isn't this wonderful?" she sighed, breathing in the warm, damp air. The moon was low. The sky bore the faintest brush of dawn across the horizon of trees to the east.

"Damn," Hal said. "Forgot my jacket. Back in a minute. Stay here—okay?" Kate nodded and watched him swing away from her. Then she turned back to the railing, looked at the shore, and let her thoughts drift back to the charades game. Hal had had such a funny look on his face when she's said "Sea Biscuit." She wondered why—surely everyone knew of the famous racehorse. But what had really astonished her was how well they'd worked together as a team, miming oceans and ovens and baking dough to reach their goal.

Kate looked at the pale trees as her thoughts moved back to her law practice in San Francisco, to the clients like Mrs. Hanneford in her housing war. Kate cared deeply about her clients' battles and her own part in the final outcome. But at this moment she could also feel her exhaustion, as though the legal warfare had used her up. Time out, she said to herself, time out.

An owl hooted. The lightening shore was thick with cottonwoods hung with vines, and Kate sighed, loving the soupy, sweet air.

"I'm back," Hal said softly.

Kate turned, feeling a quiet thrill.

"You startled me," she murmured, running a hand over her hair.

The remaining moonlight glinted on his angular face. He leaned against the rail, his ruffled shirt unbuttoned at the top, his tie on either side of the collar. He held his jacket from the crook of one finger over his shoulder.

"These are long nights for you," she said.

"Usually only the first one. People get revved up to try everything. But tomorrow night everyone will be tired out."

"I didn't know they stopped the boat at night," Kate said. "Why is that?"

"It's the only way to keep the boat safe. Old Miss is really treacherous to navigate. Pilots used to memorize every foot and turn and sandbar. The river keeps changing. Trees fall into it and lie just below the surface. They used to poke the belly out of the occasional poorly directed boat."

"So it stops at night."

"Right—chock a tree tie in."

"Is that what it's called?"

"Yes. There are lots of special terms for the river. I don't know all of them, but Andy does. If you're interested, we might have a cup of coffee with him before you get to St. Louis."

"I'd like that. You weren't born on the river, then?" she asked, thinking that the conversation was becoming more and more strained. What had happened to their earlier camaraderie? She saw him stiffen slightly and switch his jacket to his other hand.

"No, not to this life. Worth respecting, though."

His elbow, leaning on the rail, was within a hair of touching hers, and she could feel the heat of his body.

"Where were you born?"

"Kentucky. Near the eastern border."

"You grew up there, went to college there?"

"Never went to college," he said.

"Well, some say it's greatly overrated. Are your parents still alive?"

"No." He turned to look at her. "Why the interrogation, Ms. Attorney?"

"I'm sorry," she said quickly. "It's just habit. And"— she looked up at him—"curiosity."

"Well, if you're curious, Ms. Sewell, my parents were farmers. They owned very little except a patch of hard land and we worked like dogs on it. None of us went to college—we worked."

"But you—"

"Ah, yes. I had ambition. All I ever wanted to do was raise racing horses. Probably not much to you— but means a great deal to me."

She touched his arm. "Why are you so angry?"

"Because I suspect you already knew all of this—"

"How could I?" she interrupted.

"*You* tell *me*." He glared at her. For the first time she saw he was not just a glib charmer. He had power behind his pleasing facade. She stared at him, trying to sort out a mixture of feelings about him. Suddenly she remembered.

"Do you think I knew something about you because I chose Sea Biscuit for the charade?"

"It did occur to me."

"But that was pure chance."

He looked at her doubtfully.

"It just popped into my head and I said it. How *could* I know?"

"You might have run around the boat asking questions. It's happened before. And Nancy Lee's at your table."

When she had touched him a few moments before, she had quickly released him, but now she put a hand on his arm and kept it there.

"I would like to know about you—what you do, what your hopes are, how you feel about things. But I have no way of knowing anything about you unless you tell me." He was so very wary, but she couldn't imagine why. The whole conversation had taken a sudden and baffling turn. Who would care if Nancy Lee or anyone else had told her that his big ambition was to race horses?

"What's the big secret?" she asked gently. "Wouldn't *you* like to know more about *me*?"

His hands folded around her arms. "Yes. Yes, I would. Of course I would." His dark eyes caressed her face in a way that now seemed so dearly familiar.

Very slowly he stroked her cheek with his open palm.
The touch of his gaze was almost as physical as his
hand. "I'm too fast on the trigger sometimes." He
ran a hand down her cheek in a curiously touching
way. "Oh, you are so lovely and smart. I like that in
you. Don't ever get dumb."

"No chance." She could feel her smile widen.

Behind them a door opened and a couple emerged
in jogging suits.

"Good morning," they cried in unison with the
joggers' jubilance.

Kate pulled back from Hal slightly, but his hand
still held her elbow. She noticed for the first time
that it was now fully dawn. Over the river, ribbons of
color smeared the sky and a thin mist rose from the
water.

"Let's have coffee on my terrace," she said, want-
ing to prolong the moment.

Early-riser coffee—thick and black with heavy
cream— was served in the forward lounge not fifty
feet away from them. Hal swiped a pot and cream,
and she gathered up the cups as soon as the steward
set them out.

"Do you take cream?" she asked when they had
pushed open the door to the small veranda and had
seated themselves outside her room.

"No."

"I don't either." They laughed, then fell silent,
sipping the steaming coffee. Kate let her eyes travel
over the water to give her emotions time to calm
down. She mustn't let this go to her head, she warned
herself.

"I have a filly," he said, not looking at her.

"Really? What color?"

"A bay, beautiful brown. Her name is Lady Lydia."

And he began to talk. He worked on the boats to earn money for the stabling and training costs her winning purses didn't cover. Lady Lydia had won races, though, and foolishly, perhaps—he laughed— he'd borrowed on everything he had to enter her in stakes races—including the Kentucky Derby.

"You did *what*? I mean," she hastily corrected herself, amazed at his audacity, "isn't that a race only for . . ."

"For rich people and great horses. That's right. And plenty of people counseled me against it," he admitted, "because it takes dough to enter. And it's a real long shot for her because she hasn't won *that* many races. But she's won her share. And she's ready. It's her chance—I just know it. It's her hour to win."

"You work hard for a dream," Kate breathed, thinking of all the different faces he'd presented to her in the last twenty-four hours: public relations, gambler, actor, now the owner of a racehorse set to run in the Kentucky Derby.

"That's all that counts, finally. Hard work and a little luck. That helps" he added.

The sun was up and the shore sparkled on the dew-wet trees.

"It's going to be a beautiful day," he said. "It will be even better when we reach Oak Alley. Get some rest. I want to take you there."

He was on his feet and moving away with the liquid, confident, slim-hipped grace she now saw was totally his own. He opened the inner door of her stateroom, which led to the hall. There he paused and looked back. Her legs felt weak and the palms of her hands were damp. She wanted him to stay.

As though he read her heart's desire, he said, "Not now. Get some rest." He leaned toward her, put an open palm along the throbbing vein in her neck, and brushed her mouth with his. The gesture fired her senses and sent a delicate tremor down her spine and around her ribs. His hand moved up from her neck, cupping her jaw lightly. She stepped into his arms and felt them descend like wings, curling around her protectively; she felt her own arms rise to embrace the lean, hard frame that pressed gently yet persistently against her. Their lips met and held, tugged at each other. She heard him sigh and felt his warm breath brushing her cheek.

She gripped his back and felt his thighs push forward to hers. They were entangled and the pace of their movements, reaching out for each other to touch and taste, raced, accelerating her pulse. She felt light-headed and she opened her mouth as his tongue swept her lips, then plunged inside her mouth. Deep inside her, she felt a rising, glowing heat that made her breathless. She hadn't felt this way in years.

He withdrew, moved a hand in her hair, kissed her lightly on the lips. And then he was gone.

She lay in bed with the covers over her, but she couldn't sleep. She was still too caught up in the new sensations of being romantically attuned to another human being, and one about whom she knew so little, too. It thrilled her.

She stretched out languorously and tried to remember when she had been so stirred. Serenely, she felt the tentacles of memory casting back. No one had made her ache this way since Rick, on her prom night. They had gyrated to the din of the music and had clasped each other during the slower songs, swaying sensually under the colored lights and bobbing balloons and banners that laced the huge hall.

Prom night in Santa Rosa was much as it was anywhere else, she imagined. She had not thought of Rick for years. He had been from a different part of town; his parents managed a hotel. But he'd had a flashy, almost reckless air that had drawn her eye. She'd been amazed when he'd asked her to the prom, and even more surprised at herself when she'd accepted immediately.

After the dance they had driven out of town to look at the falls—a slender, perpendicular stream of water crashing from a ridge about three hundred feet above the old highway. They had driven through the sweet June night heading for it, and with the faulty but often dramatic editing of memory, she recalled having sat close to him with a rising and tremulous excitement. It was the same ecstasy that fired her imagination now, for like that long-ago boy, Hal met her on some different and deeper plane of her attention and her longing. Confidence was one trait they shared, but also a cavalier disregard for other people's prohibitions. It wasn't that Hal was selfish or uncaring—far from it. But men of his type had a sense of themselves no one could dampen. It made them tender toward others, not indifferent.

Now, in her stateroom, as the majestic wedding-cake boat throbbed along the river, moving upstream again, she allowed herself to feel her awakening to Hal.

Chapter Three

❧

On the sun deck, the bright sun spangled the water in the pool as the cheery bathers romped and splashed. Other merrymakers from the night before nursed their hangovers in deck chairs, eyes closed, faces tilted upward to receive the balmy cure of the sun's warmth.

Kate took it all in, then leaned on the rail. Cane fields stretched in all directions, domed by a brilliant blue sky. It was hard for her to believe that a short vacation could be such a delight. She could feel the knots inside her unraveling.

"How do you like my river?"

Kate turned dreamily. Nancy Lee stood at her elbow looking out at the distant shore. "Always changing, isn't it?"

"I like your river," Kate said briskly. "Though I didn't expect it to be so muddy. It's perfectly opaque—like a dark wet cloud on the ground."

Nancy Lee laughed. "You going on the tour this afternoon?"

"Should I?" Kate teased, having every intention of taking Hal up on his invitation.

"Oh, of course. It's lovely. And there's nothing like the Oaks."

"What's the name of the mansion there?"

"Bon Séjour. 'Good sojourn,' it means. Beautifully kept up, too. You must go."

"Actually I *was* planning to go, and I . . . I ran into Hal Lewis last night after the charades. He said he might accompany me, show me around."

"He's a nice fellow, isn't he?" said Nancy Lee. "Good guide, too."

"Do you know much about him?" Kate asked carefully, gazing out at the light brown river.

"Nope. Comes from Tennessee or Kentucky, I think. Sounds like it, anyway. Got a lot of style, I'd say."

"For a farmer's son, yes, he does," said Kate.

"Yup. Poor boy. Knows a lot about horses. Said he had one when we got to talkin' last trip." Kate sensed Nancy Lee eyeing her.

"He did?" Kate turned to her.

"Yes, committed to a real risky life, I'd say."

Hitch, in shorts, polo shirt, and cap, waved at them from across the deck.

"Come on, you two—don't you want to see the Oaks?"

They crossed to him and Kate saw Hitch give Nancy Lee a squeeze around the waist. "Don't need to show *you*," he said good-naturedly to Nancy Lee, "but *you've* never seen them," he added to Kate. "And neither have I." He laughed jovially.

In the distance, Kate could just barely see a line of dark green painted on the light green fields. The darker line stretched straight up from the river through the field toward an area shaded by trees and shrubs. The roof of a large house peaked above them, crowned by a belvedere. It all looked rather ordinary to Kate, even the line of dark green trees to the house, and she said so.

"You wait," chirped Nancy Lee. Her round, open face looked up at Kate and seemed to bring the sunshine with her. "You just wait."

The boat sidled up to the little dock at the levee, men threw the stage down, and people trooped over it, heading for Bon Séjour. But Kate saw no sign of Hal.

As the last stragglers stepped off the stage onto the shore, Kate had an urge to join them—especially when Hitch waved at her. But Kate had said she'd wait, and she was going to. She stared at the muddy river, the color of clay, trying hard not to be irritated or angry or hurt. Perhaps she had made too much of last night—perhaps she had been alone too long, she chided herself, and couldn't distinguish a real invitation from politeness anymore. Oh, but she wanted him to appear, take her arm, and spend the afternoon with her. She wanted him to be as good as his word. Most of all, she wanted to nurture the feelings about him that had begun to grow in her. She wanted not to be disappointed.

At last, though, in spite of her intentions, it seemed clear there wasn't any point in waiting any longer. She'd go by herself or catch up with Nancy Lee and Hitch. Her buoyant expectations became a heavy burden.

She had just stepped off the stage, feeling giddily off-balance for her first moment on land in almost a day, when she heard heavy footsteps running down the stage behind her.

"*Kate.*"

She turned. It was Hal, his expression a mixture of a frown and a smile, his red hair glinting in the sun, a blue jacket tossed over his shoulders. He took her arm gently.

"Give up on me? I was with the purser. Sorry. Glad you waited."

She was so happy to see him, her legs leaped ahead with his over the soft dirt of the levee.

"Come on. Come on." He buzzed with energy, urging her up the levee toward the column of trees, his grip on her arm strong and firm.

Suddenly he tugged at her gently and stopped.

"Put your hands over your eyes," he ordered.

"What kind of tour is this?" she asked, laughing, but she did as he said and felt his arm come around her waist to guide her.

"Just a few steps now."

His voice was deep; it rumbled close to her ear. She felt her heart quicken at his nearness. Their hips brushed against each other. Incredibly, she got a mental image of her yellow legal pad lying on her desk at a slight angle, the top page covered with her straight, firm handwriting. And she knew as she "saw" it that she was desperately fleeing from his nearness as well as from her own heightened senses.

A breeze brushed her face as she felt the air cool. Had a cloud passed over the sun? Were they now in deep shadow? The ground, she could feel, had smoothed out. A whiff of his shaving lotion and the bittersweet smell of bark came to her. He tightened his arm around her waist, then stopped walking.

"Okay—now," he whispered.

She removed her hands and gasped with pleasure. Ahead of her, on either side of the road, a double line of huge oak trees stretched before her. Their branches overlapped, creating an arch, and through the boughs streaked spikes of sunlight. At the end of the arcade, the boughs framed a pink-and-white house: Bon Séjour.

"Oh," she said, gazing at the tunnel of branches and trunks that telescoped at the end of the magical lane. "It's so—chaste."

"The trees were planted about a hundred and fifty years ago," he said, "so the owners could see the location of the house from a great distance on the river."

Kate took a step forward.

"It's very quiet under the trees, isn't it?" she remarked after a moment. The carpet of lawn spread out in a wide train beneath the trees.

"Watch the house," he murmured, drawing close to her again. "It changes color with the sun—even with the wind, it sometimes seems to me. From pale pink to a rosy red."

Slowly they walked toward the house. She could see that the long French windows were not trimmed in white, as she had at first thought, but in a soft cream. Seven columns faced the front; the lower gallery was of brick, the upper one of wood.

"You can't see it yet, but on top there's a belvedere where they could survey the cane fields," he was saying. She felt his arm creep around her waist again, sending a shudder of pleasure through her. But his words echoed in her mind.

"Yes, I saw it before. What backbreaking labor built this magic place?" she wondered aloud to him.

He nodded. "You said it. The Louisiana cane fields were killers. How did you know that?"

"I read a lot. Besides, one of my clients was the daughter of a sharecropper. At the age of eight she was sent out to the fields to start chopping. This place is such a staggering combination of terrible work and graceful accommodation, don't you think? Of slavery and abundance, I guess."

He stopped walking and smiled at her crookedly. Then he kissed her cheek gently.

They continued on, he taking her arm. The majestic arcade ended. She hated leaving its balmy shelter. The house loomed near.

"Want to go in?" he asked, bending toward her.

"No, let's stay outside a little longer."

They turned, and she looked back at the oak sentinels lining the pathway. He took her arm. "Garden, mademoiselle?" She nodded.

Honeysuckle and white Cherokee roses and ivy trailed from the roof to the ground, and as they walked along the side of the house, she saw banana and bamboo trees and budding rose bushes in a dozen colors.

"Over here," he said, urging her toward a space surrounded by Spanish-dagger shrubs. First she saw the stone bench, completely obscured from the view of the house, and then, as she moved toward it, she saw the pond. Water lilies floated on it, and from the tree above, she heard a cardinal. She sank down on the bench, facing the house, which rose above the wall of shrubs.

The columns of the house continued around the side gallery, reaching up to the roof. From her vantage point in the garden, she could see them guarding the back as well. The air was redolent with heavy, sweet honeysuckle.

"How many columns?" she asked him.

"Seven on each side. Twenty-eight in all."

She could feel his eyes on her. "What an extraordinary place," she said, gazing at the rosy house. "How can anything so pretty and idyllic have emerged from slavery?" The birds sang, and the vines of multicolored flowers climbed all the way up to the eaves.

"I don't know," he said. "Often wondered. Take a Yankee to tell us, I'm sure," he added lightly.

"Tell me more about yourself," she said.

His dark eyes studied her a moment, then he sat down.

"My life is . . . my horses. Except I have only one so far, and I'm staking everything on her," he said softly. "It is damn scary sometimes. If she doesn't finish in the money—*well*. I won't have this jacket or a toothpick of my own. I want her to win—God, how I want her to win. Do you know how rare it would be for an outsider like me to have a winner? You should see her school. That's train, get her work-outs," he added. "She just flashes by, looking so trim and neat. She's got a lot of style. She's a prancing horse." Kate watched the enthusiasm warm his eyes and his voice. "Like the winner of any race—that is, a consistent winner—she has speed, stamina, and courage."

"What a combination," she said. "Applies to people, too, doesn't it?" Hal nodded and smiled at her. "When is the derby?"

"Early May, first Saturday. It's for three-year-olds—those who survive the rugged training. Eighteen to twenty on a field."

"How long does it take to go around the track?"

"You ask good questions," he said, tilting his head at her. "To go around the field? Secretariat did it in one minute, fifty-nine seconds, but the usual time is about two minutes."

"Is it expensive to enter the race?"

"I'll say. Thousands."

"What other races has she won?"

"The Beldame, the Alabama, and a couple of others to qualify for the derby. She didn't start winning or even placing until pretty recently." He smiled puckishly. "She's really a hell of a lucky accident. She's one of a kind."

Kate knew it was very special to see someone so warmly proud. She could have hugged him but hesitated, for she heard voices coming up from the oak arcade. The tour group from the boat was upon them, she guessed.

"Hal, is that—" she began.

"Ah, there you are," cried Cynthia, coming onto the veranda in the van of the crowd. She waved to them. "Yoo-hoo. What are you doing?" she called out. "Have you seen the house yet?"

Cynthia, Kate noticed, was wearing a yellow sun dress with a short bolero jacket. Roland appeared behind her, took her arm, and led her down into the garden toward them.

"You been inside yet, Kate?" Roland asked as he and Cynthia neared Kate and Hal.

"We were just about to do that," she answered. "Hal's leading a tour."

Hal looked at her quickly, raising his eyebrows, then he shrugged and laughed. Kate looked toward the house again and saw a woman of about eighty standing on the veranda, leaning on her cane. She was straight as a stick, wore a flowered dress and red shoes, and her cheeks were lightly rouged.

"Who is she?" Kate asked Hal. Cynthia and Roland turned to stare at the woman.

"The owner—great-granddaughter of the builder," Hal said. "She usually leads the tours, by the way."

Hal rose and Kate followed, starting out of the little clearing and toward the woman. Roland and Cynthia were right behind her. As Kate walked she caught a glimpse of Hitch and Nancy Lee across the garden near a group of brilliant red roses. Hitch had changed into a searsucker suit and looked quite debonair as he took Nancy Lee's arm. Kate wished she and Hal were with them among the flowers. At that moment, as Kate mused about her newfound pleasure in Hal's company, Roland astonished her by taking her hand.

Kate disengaged herself immediately, then stopped on the stone flagging at the bottom of the steps.

"How do you do?" she greeted the old lady. "You have a most beautiful garden."

"Thank you," the woman said crisply, but she smiled. "We've managed." She had pale blue eyes and her skin looked like peach-colored velvet. "Would you all like to see the house now?"

"Oh, yes," Kate responded.

The woman shot a quick glance at her. There was warmth as well as appraisal in it.

"I'll take them in, Miss Simons," said Hal smoothly. "No need for you to trouble," he went on, coming up beside Kate. The woman smiled at him.

"How are you, Mr. Lewis?" she asked, then added, "Stick to the main rooms below, if you wouldn't mind."

Roland put an arm under Kate's elbow as Hal came up on her other side. Cynthia was trailing behind. They mounted the steps to the veranda, moving toward the tall double French doors. Inside, the house was cool, spacious, and serene.

Hal said, "There are four main rooms on each floor and they all open out on this central hallway."

The hall was more like a huge, welcoming chamber, running the length of the building. Its parquet floors gleamed. A wide staircase wound down from the upper floor. Roland led Kate into the sitting room to the left as Cynthia paused outside, and Hal waited for her. The room was furnished in antiques, most of the upholstered pieces in pale pastels. The long windows looked out on the garden.

"It's wonderful," Kate said, feeling a trifle uncomfortable with Roland. She looked back for Hal and saw Cynthia's profile just outside the door. Roland hovered, darkly courteous. "But perhaps," Kate said, "we should get back to Hal and Cynthia."

"Let me show you the mantel in this room," Roland said, moving close to her to take her arm.

"Have you been here before?" she asked.

"Yes. Once." His dark face looked flushed and heavy in spite of its cherubic features. "The mantel is a very fine example of Italian molding, sculpturing."

Kate turned back to look for Hal and Cynthia, but the hallway was empty.

"You are a most attractive woman," Roland breathed, "and I count myself lucky to be alone with you even for a moment."

"Mr. Dupuis," Kate said, moving away from him, "I do not have shipboard romances, if that's what you have in mind."

"Who said anything about romance?" he asked, smiling widely. He had, she suddenly noticed, a rather lopsided smile that, on a less overbearing man, would have been winning. "Women often jump to romantic conclusions," he intoned.

"Really, Mr. Dupuis," Kate said with exasperation, "that's a ridiculous comment. I have no illusions at all about you on that score." She moved past him to the door.

Roland caught her hand. "I apologize," he said, the courtly, Southern gentleman returning. "Please forgive me if I distressed you in any way." His voice held real feeling, which she could not ignore.

"Of course," Kate said quickly.

"Won't you call me Roland? 'Mr. Dupuis' sounds a little artificial."

"Sure," Kate agreed absently. All his pretense had vanished, and suddenly he seemed to Kate to be vulnerable.

"Can't we just be friends?" he asked.

"That's what I would prefer, too," she said. Kate looked at his hand around her wrist. He dropped his hold on her.

"Let me show you the other rooms—or would you rather catch up with Cynthia and Hal?"

"Yes, let's do that," Kate said, relieved.

In the distance, at the end of the arcade of oaks, Kate heard the steamboat's whistle blast. Most of the passengers were ahead of her, but she dawdled along, enjoying the cool alley of majestic boughs and sturdy trunks. It was hard to let the beautiful sight of them go, yet with every step she neared the end of the corridor.

The wonderful, though brief time with Hal remained with her. Still, Kate wondered at his new attentions to Cynthia, with whom he now walked near the head of the returning group. As palpably as she felt the nearness of the sheltering trees, she recalled his embrace of the night before and her own amazing reactions. How much she would like to be walking with him now.

Nancy Lee and Hitch came up to her. "Isn't this a wonderful day, and isn't it a glorious house?" Nancy Lee asked eagerly.

"Yes, and yes," said Kate. She didn't quite know what to say. Yes, it is a great day and, yes, it is a beautiful house. But also, yes, it was built in an ugly time. It all sounded harsh.

"Even I liked it and I hate tours," Hitch chimed in. He winked at Kate. "Where's your fiery gambler?"

"He's not mine," Kate replied zestfully.

"Oh, pardon me," Hitch moaned, grinning.

"He's somewhere ahead with the Southern belle," Nancy Lee said. She never seemed to miss anything. "He's not supposed to show favoritism to any one passenger or to become involved with any one of us," she said pointedly to Kate. "If he's caught, he'll get the sack."

"Get the sack," roared Hitch. "God, I haven't heard that one for years. It means," he said, turning to Kate, "getting fired."

"I know what it means, Hitch. Like getting canned."

"Well, he would," persisted Nancy Lee. "Lots of the stewards on board are called to rooms for no good reason—other than hanky-panky, that is. And the *doctor* . . ." She let out a long, shrill whistle.

"Well, Hal's in no danger of getting fired as far as I'm concerned," Kate said.

"Too bad," said Hitch mournfully.

Kate looked at him and laughed out loud. "What kind of law do you do?" Hitch asked.

"Public service—antidiscrimination cases, the elderly, tenants' rights."

"Oh—so you are *useful*."

"I hope so." She saw Hal slow his pace and drop back from Cynthia, who had been joined by Roland.

In a moment Hal was next to Kate just as Hitch asked her, "Ever think of getting married?"

"Sure," she said. "Marriage and a law practice are not mutually exclusive. Do you think they might be?"

"Nope, not me," said Hitch.

"I don't, either," said Hal, smiling at them. Then he asked Kate, "Why'd you become a lawyer?"

"Because I thought I could make a difference. Can't just go through life without leaving some kind of track, can you?"

"Oh, you'd be surprised how many people do," Hal said, his warm eyes glancing across her face. "Not a sign that they've been around. But, then, you're different."

Kate looked at Hal, responding to him. She thought of her life in San Francisco. How distant Hal's life was from hers and hers from his among the stables and horses. She was everything urban and he was everything rural in this country. Their lives, she suddenly feared, would never fit together.

Hal leaned toward her and whispered, "Can you join me later tonight?" His fingertips brushed against her hand. She shelved all her doubts about their differences as she passionately anticipated the next time she could see him.

Chapter Four

Kate looked forward to seeing Hal more than she cared to admit. Indeed, it was practically all she could think of. But, after Nancy Lee's warning, she didn't want to be too obvious, so instead of playing poker at his table, Kate joined her dinner partners for the singles party in the forward lounge. Perhaps, she thought, the activity would get her mind off her meeting later on with Hal.

The small combo was loud and cheery. A mood of high anticipation—perhaps, Kate thought, for new if transitory relationships—permeated the packed lounge. At the door, she was given five tickets, a different number on each one.

"These are to ensure that singles meet other singles," Cynthia said, cruising the room a little nearsightedly. She had taken her glasses off and Kate once again noticed the woman's delicate profile. "The numbers will be called during the party."

"I don't get it," Kate said.

"When your number is called, there will be a man with the same number and you have that dance together."

"Oh." Kate glanced at Nancy Lee. "Well, what won't they think of next." She laughed, putting Cynthia on a little.

Cynthia tossed an assessing glance at Kate that probably looked sharper than it was meant to be. "You really haven't been on a boat before, have you?" Cynthia drawled.

Before Kate could answer, the cruise director stepped to the microphone. He had a wholesome smile and an air of "Let's all pull together now and have a great time." He read off the first set of numbers.

"I got one," Kate said. "What do I do now?"

Her question was answered immediately as the cruise director explained the system.

"All those whose number I just called step to this side of the room," he was saying.

Kate did as directed, deciding that she would stay for one dance. Most of all, she wanted to go into the other lounge, where she could see Hal. She felt the color rise to her cheeks as she thought of him, memory following memory.

There was the first moment she saw Hal as he walked through the hotel lobby with that almost imperceptibly seductive gait. And the way he'd turned from the front desk to appraise her as she'd approached him. She wanted so much to be with him now. As the music washed the room with sound, she let the eddies and undertones of conversation around her fade, freeing her for private visions, private desires. The tingling touch of Hal's lips the night before returned to her, and the warm enclosure of his arms. What plan did he have in mind that would allow them to meet this night? Could she help him arrange it? Should she even try?

Kate came out of her reverie to see she had been surrounded by a score of people whose numbers had been called. Many of the women were laughing a little shrilly; the men were stoically scanning the field. Kate caught herself looking around for Hal, even though she knew he wasn't there.

"Now you ladies will be chosen by the men for this dance," cried the director over the hubbub.

This is silly, Kate thought as she surveyed the field of men.

She didn't want to dance with anyone—but Hal.

She was just heading toward the door when she felt a tap on her shoulder.

"Not leaving already?"

It was Roland.

"Yes. I'm very tired, and the noise—"

"Just stay for one dance," he pressed her.

"I didn't think your number was up," she managed to say.

"I switched with Nancy Lee."

She'll pay for this, Kate thought as the band started to play and Roland whirled her onto the floor.

He was a surprisingly good dancer, light on his feet and graceful. She was pleased to find that although he held her close, his embrace was no tighter than was appropriate to the dance. Still, she did not wish to encourage him, and she looked straight ahead over his shoulder.

"I regret causing you any discomfort this afternoon," he began, whisking her around the floor.

"You didn't. Don't worry about it."

"I'd like to begin again. Would you join me for a glass of champagne? There's a free table over there in the corner."

"Just one, Roland. Then I really must leave."

But what would she do in her room? Dream about

Hal, that's what she'd do. She braced herself, ready to be distracted, no matter how momentarily.

"Tell me about your work and what you like most about it," he said when they were seated and the champagne had been ordered. He looked at her earnestly.

She launched into a description of her law practice, but midway, she saw his eyes glaze over, a look she knew. He was trying to be polite, but she'd learned that "the glaze" was a sign that its owner would soon take his own turn to speak. In this case she was actually curious to see what would be said. Roland's lines and maneuvers should be quite polished from practice, if she was any judge. She decided to throw something outrageous into her monologue to test the quality of his attention.

"I look on the law only as a way to advance my real ambition, which is to be an engineer. Building bridges is what excites me most." Roland was nodding, a fixed smile on his face. "I'm thinking of joining the Army Corps of Engineers next winter."

Roland downed his champagne. "Army, eh? Army and law?" He looked baffled. "Well, of course I'm just a country boy." His eyes became shrewd. "You *are* a handful."

A steward came up to them. "Miss Sewell?" he asked. Kate nodded. "There's a call for you. If you will follow me?"

It must be Hal, she thought excitedly. She excused herself and followed the steward out of the noisy room.

"Just down this way," he said, "and make a left at the stairs." She thanked him.

An instant after making the turn, she found herself in Hal's arms. "It's my own form of ambush," he said, holding her gently. They were in an alcove under the stairs.

"I see." She smiled. "And the steward is your cousin."

"Nope. Merely a good friend."

"I was just thinking of you," she admitted, feeling his body close to hers and breathing in the smell of his hair. "Are you on a coffee break?" He nodded. "Too bad. I think Cynthia just deserted the singles party to play cards," Kate said, half teasing, half questioning.

"She's very pretty, it's true," Hal said slowly, holding Kate close.

"And very smart, too. She's in banking, you know."

"I know. But she's not the one I'm with, is she?"

Kate shook her head sheepishly. "No, she's not. And I'm glad." She was pressed against him, feeling his arms bind her. She tilted her head back and brushed her lips against his as though to test his reaction. His lips parted, responding warmly, and she gave away her intense joy at seeing him with the trembling passion of her kiss. One of his hands moved into her hair, cupping the back of her head gently as she felt herself swimming in the deep pond of her desire for him. They broke apart only to press together again, both unwilling to surrender their newfound intimacy and all the sensations that sprang from it. His mouth was moist and warm, his tongue a gentle invader, soothing her pounding heart. Once again, reluctantly, they drew apart.

"Oh, Hal," she breathed.

"Meet me later?" he said hoarsely. She nodded, not trusting her ability to speak. "I have a surprise for you," he added, smoothing back her hair with one hand. His eyes found hers, and even in the dim alcove, Kate could see the tension of desire in them.

Reluctantly she parted from him and walked to the set of stairs that would take her to her stateroom. She wanted to return with him to the larger lounge, where she could luxuriate in watching him from a distance. Maybe, she thought, I could get a little distance on my emotions that way. Even as she contemplated this she knew she didn't really want any distance. She was compelled toward closeness and connection.

But as she closed the door of her stateroom behind her, she knew she was too keyed up to nap. She went out on the veranda. The huge paddle wheel was stilled, the boat secured for the night. The air was warm and moist; the sounds of the crickets and marsh birds carried over the vast river. She leaned back, folded her arms behind her head, and closed her eyes.

It was some time later that she heard the knock at her door, very faintly. Was she imagining it? No, the knock came again. She felt her pulse quicken.

It was Hal.

He was wearing a cap, pulled down dashingly over one eye, and a light green jacket. "I hope I'm not too late. May I come in?"

She nodded wordlessly and stood aside. "Nancy Lee told me that you'll get in trouble if—"

Hal waved her words away. "Some things are worth the risks." He smiled warmly, his eyes lingering on her face. "Will you come with me?"

"Where are you going?" she asked, though she knew she would go wherever he asked her. Even the sweet anticipation of seeing him had not prepared her for the joy of being with him.

"Into the bayou. I've planned a little excursion for us." Quiet enthusiasm glowed on his face. "I've got a skiff tied up below and two strong arms and—" They stood about three feet apart. Now he reached out and took her in his arms. "And a beautiful woman who's never seen a bayou. It's all arranged."

"Isn't this a little odd? I mean, two people out in a little boat at night. Is it safe?"

"I wouldn't take you anywhere it wasn't safe."

"How'd you put all this together?"

"Easy, counselor. Remember I said I know the pilot of this boat, Andy Tobias—the one who got me this job?"

"And got you the skiff, too?"

"In a way." He grinned.

"But you'll be fired if we're caught," she whispered as they made their way down to the lower level of the boat.

"Andy won't fire me," he whispered back, his dark eyes flashing. "The management will."

The little skiff, which looked just like a rowboat to her, was fitted out with cushions and blankets at one end. It was thrilling and secret and forbidden. The pungent smell of the river hung about them like a curtain; the riverboat, from her new, lower perspective in the skiff, loomed over them like a huge building.

He pulled on the oars and guided the boat along the dark shore. She leaned back against the pillows and stared up at the starry sky. An owl hooted.

"See up there?" he asked, indicating a spot in the river ahead of them.

She turned. The shoreline opened and soon they were deep inside a narrow waterway. Huge trees hung with moss bent over the still water, and a bird she could not identify called out mournfully.

"This is the last of the bayou land," he said. "By tomorrow we'll be up to St. Francisville." He leaned on the oars and let the boat drift. The shape of the trees emerged from the shadows as the moon nudged through the tallest branches.

"This is so peaceful," she sighed.

The boat knocked gently against the edge of the natural waterway. "We'll stop here," he murmured. "Don't want to go too far—especially at night."

He tied the little boat to a large, exposed root, then carefully made his way back to her. Leaning against a cushion, he asked, "Refreshments?" He reached out for the brandy flask and then produced two small glasses, filling each with brandy. Then he opened a tin and offered her a cookie. She laughed at his careful preparations.

"Do you take these little excursions on every trip?" she asked, biting into the cookie.

"No. But I've thought of it."

He stretched out next to her, rocking the boat slightly. "To your good health, counselor," he toasted her, raising his glass.

She sipped the brandy, feeling the bite of it on her tongue. His nearness against the cushions stirred her. His head was tilted up and away from her in profile as he gazed into an overhanging tree. He held his glass in one hand; the other was folded behind his head.

"Tell me more about your filly," she said.

"Ah," he sighed and, still staring into the shadowy

bayou, said softly, "She's a distance runner—not a sprinter."

"Did you buy her?"

"In a way. I was working around the stables of a big training outfit, and I bought the mare for five hundred dollars. Beautiful old mare, way past her prime, but such a sweet nature and good lines. She had had a couple of good colts, too, that had paid their way in purses. It had always been a dream of mine to own racehorses, and I thought I'd better get going on it, start somewhere, though I had no right to such a dream since I had no money."

"Everyone has a right to his dreams," Kate said.

"That's what I kept telling myself. But sometimes it's hard to be the only person who believes in you." Hal turned to look at her. "I think you know about that, too, don't you?" She nodded, feeling her heart contract.

"Anyway," he went on, his voice low, "the stable owner was a friend and he gave me free stud service with Roustabout. Lady Lydia was the result. But my mare died about a month after my filly was born.

"What did you do?" Kate asked.

"I got a special milk mixture from the vet and I fed her myself. I lived in her shed for months. She knows me better than I know myself—and I sure do know her."

No wonder this filly was everything to him, she thought. "But what made you think she was a racehorse?"

"Well, of course, at that age you don't know, but she had good breeding, good lines, and, most of all, she had a good personality."

"Personality?"

"Mm-hm. Horses are all different. They like to eat different things, and they run different and they talk different, and they *are* different. If that surprises you, you have a lot to learn about horses."

The rich smells of the bayou and the compelling presence of the man caught at her. "What makes you think I'll learn?" Kate whispered, almost afraid to look at him.

"Couldn't say," he replied. His eye narrowed a little and the moonlight glanced off his brow as he moved. "Everyone likes Lady Lydia—she's a looker and she's smart. I never allowed anyone to take the stick to her, and most of the time I schooled her myself. She's won some races and she's going to win a lot more. You wait till you meet her—" He broke off, checking his remark. It had startled her, too.

"Well, I'd love to, of course, but I—"

He put a finger to her lips and turned fully toward her for the first time since mooring the little boat. His face was in shadows, but she felt his eyes upon her as his hand slipped down around her shoulders to draw her close.

"Let's not talk. You sometimes use words to keep your distance," he said softly.

"I do?"

He nodded. In the next moment his head moved over her, blocking the stars, and in the next, his lips found hers, tenderly nuzzling and exploring, then slipped away to brush her cheek.

"I have done nothing all day but think of you," he said, clasping his arm around her waist and pressing her closer to him.

"I'm so glad to hear that," she whispered.

Suddenly she recognized she'd lived with a hunger

a long time without knowing it. Now it clutched at her. She reached out for him, kissing his cheek as her awakened desire streaked down her spine. She pressed herself against him fervently and a sigh escaped her. The boat swayed in the water as they kissed desperately, longingly, holding nothing back. Her desire for him was like a waterfall inside her, tumbling and roaring.

"Undress, please," she said softly, loosening her hold on him.

He released her and leaned against the side of the boat, his arms outspread. "An immoderate wish." He smiled at her.

"Very. I am not known for my moderation."

His expression changed abruptly, and he reached out for her again, as though seized with longing.

"I can't stop touching you," he whispered. Holding her close, he pressed one hand against the small of her back as the other unbuttoned her blouse. The night was so warm that the moisture from his lips as he kissed her breasts and traced his tongue across the soft mounds felt cool. She lay back upon the pillows and opened her arms for him.

"You are lovely," he whispered, looking into her eyes and brushing the back of his hand on her cheek. The restraint of the gesture inflamed her. "I want you so much," he said.

She felt she would never be the same again, that she was changed, bolder, that she had met her match and that her desire mirrored his.

"Undress," she said again, breathily, reaching for the buttons on his shirt, then sliding her hand inside. She wondered at the way the mere touch of his chest seemed to escalate her fever for him. She wanted

their first exploration of each other—now inevitable—
to go on forever, and, at the same time, she wanted
to taste its final, ripe fruit immediately. Hal began to
slip out of his shirt.

His shoulders gleamed darkly in the shadows, well
muscled and lean. Slowly she moved her eyes from
them to his face, and then, practicing the same restraint as he, she looked up into the sky and at the
shadows of the trees as she felt him wriggling out of
his trousers. The boat rolled uneasily, but her sense
of safety was perfectly placid. At last he sank down
beside her and reached for the sash to her skirt, then
unfolded it, peeling the garment away from her.
Kissing his way down her body, he drew her half slip
down her thighs and legs. Still she did not move but
held her gaze upon the stars and let the delicious
tongues of fire lick at her.

The moon had floated to a spot in the sky un-
shielded by trees, and it made the little glade where
they lay glow softly. Hal was moving up her body
now, his lips glancing across her skin, sliding upward
over her breasts and neck. Then his face was next to
hers and she could feel the warm breath of him. She
shifted her gaze from the stars to meet his extraordinary eyes. His lips were smiling but his eyes held a
look far more serious.

"What is it?" Kate asked.

"I want to be so careful with you . . ."

"Don't be. I'm a woman, not a china doll."

"That's not what I mean," he said.

"What do you mean?" she whispered.

"I want . . ." he began, then paused. She ran her
fingertips across his muscular arms.

"What?" she urged.

"I want . . . to share everything with you without holding back, without inhibition. I want us truly to be together. Nothing between . . . nothing. And without words. I don't want you . . ." he said so softly she could hardly hear him, "to look away from me for a moment."

Kate felt herself soaring with his words and all that they implied. This was no ordinary man and this would be no ordinary night.

She leaned toward him and kissed him fully upon the mouth, sucking at his lower lip, then pulling away and looking at him. Slowly he lowered his lips to her neck and traced a line to her breast, drawing his tongue across her hardened nipple, lingering there. She groaned and clasped her arms around his naked back.

"I want to look at you," she said.

He drew away. Mutely they gazed at each other. The heat radiated from him. A star of emotion burst within her as she leaned to kiss his lips, which held a hint of brandy. His teeth found her earlobe. She felt she was plunging into a deep silver pool that made her thighs tingle and part as she felt him lying against her without urgency but with desire.

He had one arm around her, his lips still close to her ear; she heard him say, "I know what you need. I know . . . you. I know you . . ." His firm, sensitive hands reached out for her and swept her from neck to thighs; he was not afraid to touch her anywhere, yet she felt no sense of invasion.

"Tell me with your eyes," she heard him saying.

From habit, Kate tried to gather words together, but that seemed, for the first time, impossible.

"You already know," she said at last.

"Look at me."

Their eyes locked. He was making love to her with his eyes and she had never before seen or felt such contact. It was as hopeless to stop the penetration of his eyes as that of his body—and she was far from wishing either would cease. Perhaps he felt at that moment that his eyes held her as palpably as his arms, for he released one arm from her waist. She was no less bound to him and he acknowledged it, then dipped his head to plumb her mouth.

As she spun into a spiral of widening ecstasy, no longer afraid the boat would capsize, indeed, no longer aware of even being in the little boat, she saw the shadow of a luminous white ibis skim across the tree-lined shore. It dipped one huge white wing, then floated out across the dark, warm river as Hal nuzzled gently inside her, lacing their bodies, binding their desires, his eyes never leaving her face.

As she climbed the rope ladder up the side of the vast steamboat, she felt as weak as a rag. Her wrists, especially, seemed to have no strength, and a delicious lassitude spilled over her like dew. Hal gave her a boost, and she climbed aboard. He drew her into his arms and she felt again the pungent reward of being with him.

"Sweet Kate," he whispered.

Surrounded by his embrace, she was looking over his shoulder when she noticed a faint, quick motion at the side of the stairway. A flash of yellow came next, and for a split second Kate thought she saw Cynthia's sharp, delicate face. Then Hal's hand slipped under Kate's chin, pulling her lips toward his, sliding his tongue inside her mouth as his thighs rubbed gently against hers. Kate forgot about Cynthia.

Chapter Five

❧

It was the silence that awoke her. Some inner consciousness warned her that the boat, which was supposed to be moving, was not.

She opened her eyes. It was daylight. Distantly she heard the calls of people, as though from land. She stretched and felt the muscles ripple down her back and legs. She raised her arms above her head and gripped the antique brass bedstead. "Oh," she sighed, "oh, I feel so good."

Sitting bolt upright, she ran her hands through her hair and peered across the room at her reflection in the mirror. Then the wave of memories from last night flooded her warmly, and she lay back on the pillows to enjoy them.

Never had she felt so encompassed by the strength of another human being, or so loved. His image rose before her eyes again. She saw him with a sheer film of dampness on his face and shoulders from the humid river, felt his lips tenderly parting hers, nibbling at her, tugging delicious sensations from her, one by one. Enchanted with the romance of the dark, mysterious bayou and the sunny, loving man beside her, she also recalled that his candor and boldness had stitched the night's special fabric. He seemed to have an uncanny understanding of her, a complete acceptance of the woman and the person inside her. It had made her feel safe, and she reveled in it now.

She jumped out of bed and plucked at the blinds. The boat was tied to a levee in the midst of a glaringly bright day.

St. Francisville. Of course. How long had they been there? She glanced at the clock: it was after two in the afternoon. Hastily Kate began to dress. She wanted to see the historic St. Francisville but, even more, she wanted to see the angular, dark-eyed, redheaded man who had made her feel so wanted, accepted. At the thought of seeing him again; touching him, a thousand butterflies rose in her stomach.

Outside, dressed in slacks and a blouse, Kate leaned over the rail, looking at the town—a collection of houses and buildings and roads laced with the sweet greenery peculiar to the South.

"Good morning." It was Roland, smiling down at her. "Did you have a pleasant night?"

She looked up at him, wondering if Cynthia had mentioned having seen her at three in the morning. But there was no mischievous, knowing expression on his face. She saw only a determined desire to be her companion.

"Yes," she responded pleasantly, "I slept very well, thank you."

"Are you going on the tour to Rosedown?"

"Oh, I thought I'd just go into town—that's about all," she fibbed shamelessly, hoping to discourage him.

"What? And miss the gardens where Audubon did

his famous sketches?" He took her arm. It was, she saw, useless to resist.

In town, as they were trying to locate the bus tour to the mansion on a street close to the river, she saw Hal. He was getting into a jitney with Cynthia. Nancy Lee and Hitch and another man she didn't know were right behind him.

"Come on," Kate cried out to Roland, "that's *it*." She ran ahead of the astonished man to hold the jitney.

"I'm sorry, miss, there's not a seat left," the driver said as she stepped aboard. Roland was right behind her.

"Here's one," said Hal, rising. He was sitting next to Cynthia. Kate made her way down the aisle toward him, feeling the blush start from her toes. A slow, deliberate smile widened his lips as she approached, and he held her shamelessly with his probing eyes. She brushed against him as she sat down. The touch was like a branding. Roland, not pleased, sat down on the other side of his sister, who was craning her neck to look at Hal. The door closed, and the jitney jerked into action.

Nancy Lee was next to Kate; on the other side of her was the man she didn't know. Hal now stood over her, hanging onto a bar. Kate saw Hal's eyes slip toward her and she smiled up at him.

"Kate," he said, "I don't think you know Andy Tobias, our pilot."

Tobias, about fifty, could have been Hal's father in size and build. His hair was nearly white, but his eyebrows were jet black, arching over kindly, milky-blue eyes that reminded her of queenie marbles.

"Howdy." His voice was gruff and low as he smiled.

"Glad to meet you," Kate said. And to Hal, "Do we have the whole crew with us today? Who's minding the boat?"

"Not me," said Andy, chortling a little.

"I thought it would be a good idea for Andy to take a couple of hours and see the most beautiful garden in the South. Too long at the helm, you know."

"I've only seen it twice before," Andy said, winking at her.

"I'd kinda like to stay in town," Hitch remarked to Nancy Lee. "I've seen enough mansions."

"Oh, this will only take an hour. And I want to show you Henry Clay's gothic bedroom suite," said Nancy Lee.

"Well, that's a bit of news," he said, smiling at her broadly.

Hal stood over Kate; their eyes met again. Kate wanted to tell him how she felt about their private interlude in the skiff, and what heady rivulets of warmth he'd sent running through her. "St. Francisville was where half the millionaires in the U.S. in the nineteenth century lived," was all that she could finally come up with.

"Is that right?" Hal said, his voice rumbling deep in his chest and his eyes alight. He said the words as though he really meant, Does your body feel as good as mine?

The jitney rolled out of town and wound through the woods until it came to a white gate. Kate stood aside as everyone got off, hoping Hal would join her, but he was talking with the jitney driver. Andy came up to her.

"Want to walk ahead a bit?" she asked him.

"Okay," Andy said laconically. "Good to stretch my legs. Guess that's what Hal had in mind."

The driveway was about four hundred feet long. On either side, among the trees, vases and stone urns were stationed. Through the tree boughs and the hanging moss, Kate could just make out a kind of dim white cloud ahead. How odd, she thought, and then realized she was looking at the mansion.

Rosedown was not a massive house. Five facing columns and two verandas, lower and upper, seemed to float among the trees and vines.

"Have you been a pilot long?" she asked, so she wouldn't seem to be ignoring Andy.

" 'Bout thirty years. That's the mansion."

"So I see . . . It looks like a stage set. Was Hal an actor once?"

"Not to my knowledge."

"I think he's good-looking enough to have been one. Where do you know him from?"

"His mother was my sister." He rolled his eyes toward her briefly.

"You're his uncle? I didn't know that."

No response from Andy, who kept his eyes straight ahead.

"Look at *that*," cried Kate, pointing to a statue set on a pedestal nestled between the boxwoods. It was of an Indian with one foot planted on an alligator. "What a strange sculpture," she murmured, going up to it.

"That's a Louisiana alligator he's stepping on," Andy said. "I think it represents the United States. But there are others around here that represent the other continents, so I'm told."

They walked on.

"Hal talks a lot about his filly," Kate said when conversation lagged.

"Aye. They're close."

"Yes, it seems so."

Another long silence engulfed them. "I'm from San Francisco," Kate offered.

"Aye. You're an attorney."

"That's right. Did Hal mention that?" she asked, pleased that he might have done so.

"Nope. Nancy Lee did. She's a newspaper of information about passengers."

"Oh." Kate felt as she did at some depositions; it was almost impossible to get the information she sought. But what did she seek here with Andy? Surely nothing specific. It occurred to her that, in truth, she wanted him to like her.

"Did you know Hal as a little boy?"

"Nope. He wasn't born when I was a little boy." Andy's eyebrow jumped.

Kate laughed. "You know what I mean."

"Yup. And if you want to know more about Hal, you'd better ask him. No offense."

Kate pursed her lips, embarrassed. "I'm sorry. I guess I did come on a little strong, but I didn't mean anything by it. Hal's an awfully nice guy." She felt sheepish.

They went into the mansion as a group this time, craning their necks at the intricately gilded chandeliers, the painted designs on the ceilings, and the massive, airy parlors.

"Yes, sir, this is pure Louisiana," murmured Roland, who had caught up with her in the house. He put an arm around her shoulders.

"Please don't do that," Kate said quietly.

"How about a drink later?" he asked, his arm remaining on her as he steered her out of the salon into the main hall.

Kate stopped. "I said, please take your arm off my shoulders."

He laughed lightly. "Or you'll what?"

She tried to move away from the circle of his arm, but he would not allow it.

"Don't be so uppity," he whispered happily, "you've proved your point. Though, I admit, I like women with spirit."

"Then you'll love this," she said sweetly, and drove her fist into his soft stomach as hard as she could. He doubled slightly at the waist and his arm jerked away from her reflexly. A look of embarrassed amazement passed over his face.

Kate turned to head outside, her face coloring, wondering if she'd gone a little crazy. She was as furious as she could remember feeling in a long time. A buzz of words rose up behind her like bees, but she did not stop to investigate or to explain her impetuous act.

She strode down a gravel walkway and over a small bridge, deep into the heart of the garden, which had the scope of a planned woods. Lavender, magenta, and white camellias led the way past magnolia trees, a crape myrtle, and olive boughs, which were hung in moss.

Why am I so angry? she wondered, but she knew. It was his insistence that he would get his way, as well as the predatory look in his eyes. She had seen it before and had never liked it. She rounded a corner and came upon a summerhouse with trellised sides surrounded by a jumbled carpet of white violets. The deep woods pressed up behind it.

Feeling relieved by the privacy, she sat down inside on the bench. Really, it was inexcusable what she had done, she thought. At the same time, Roland was so irritating. Had Hal seen what she'd done? God, what would he think of her punching Roland? Would he laugh? Too late now. She leaned back and closed her eyes.

A twig snapped. She looked up.

Hal stood at the entrance of the summerhouse, his arms pressed on either side of the door, Samson-like. He regarded her gently with smiling eyes.

"We all wondered where you were. We fanned out over the garden." His eyes did not leave her face as they caressed her. "Is this what I can expect from you—a good punch in my solar plexus?"

"I know you will find this hard to believe—"

He laughed. "I'll believe anything now."

"I never punched anyone before."

"I don't believe you. I saw you sink your fist into him from your shoulder. That punch was premeditated."

"True. For about five seconds before it landed."

"Why'd you punch him?"

"Because he's arrogant. Because he was deeply annoying, and after I'd told him to stop what he was doing and even tried to move away from him—which he would not allow—it seemed the only solution."

Hal considered her, a faint smile playing on his lips, arms still outstretched against the doorframe. "Seem like good reasons to me."

Her hunger for him returned in a rush. "Want to step inside?" she asked.

"We should get back soon."

She went to him, put her arms around his lean waist. "Let's not go yet." She pressed against him and felt waves of pleasure wing through her. She raised her head, her lips trembling in anticipation before they met his.

"We have to get back," he said reluctantly, sweeping a lock of her hair back from her face.

"But look at this idyllic setting," she murmured, "all trellis and birds and violets."

"As good as last night?" His eyes searched her face knowingly, and she loved the intimacy of the look. She could feel the tension in him. Was it the tension of desire held in check, or eagerness to get away? She could not tell. He took her hand and led her down the path, away from the summerhouse.

In the distance, she heard the steamboat whistle.

"Doesn't that mean we have an hour or so?" she asked, resisting his hand, trying to turn him back toward the summerhouse.

He didn't answer. She put an arm about his waist.

"I was thinking—" she began.

"*Hal.*" It was Cynthia, farther down the path, by a stand of boxwood trees.

Hal grabbed Kate's hand and plunged around a camellia hedge that gave way to a bed of lilies. "Shh," he cautioned her.

She laughed. "Are we hiding?"

"Sort of," he whispered, and put his fingers to her lips. They sat down near the lilies, the spreading boughs of a magnolia above them.

"*Hal,*" came the call again.

And, from another direction, "*Hal.*" It was Hitch. "Where is he?" she heard Hitch say to someone.

"We're surrounded," Kate hissed.

"Hal. Kate." Now it was Nancy Lee calling.

Hal wrapped his arms around Kate and pressed his cheek against hers. "Looks as though I've led you into a box canyon." He grinned and hugged her tightly. "Oh, that feels so good. God, how I've missed you." She tilted her face up.

"Hal," Cynthia called again; she was nearer now.

Kate nestled into the lilies, stretching out next to him, breathing in the fragrance of ground and blossom. She felt his fingers unbutton the fastening at her neck; his hand moved inside around her breast, softly, gently.

"Hal." Cynthia was on the other side of the hedge.

"Do you see them?" asked Roland, his voice coming nearer to Cynthia's on the gravel path.

"No, I don't. Do you think they're together?"

Roland said, "Probably. You'd better give up any notion of getting close to that Hal."

"Now, Roland, you know me better than that," Cynthia said, her voice lower and stronger than usual.

Behind the hedge, Hal's lips found Kate's ear and probed gently.

"Hitch." Now it was Nancy Lee calling from another direction.

"Over here," Hitch replied from a distance.

Hal's hand freed Kate's breast from her blouse as they lay perfectly still in the lilies. He raised his head slowly, then carefully peeled away the blouse so that her other breast was also exposed. Kate could feel a smile starting deep inside her as she imagined Roland and Cynthia muttering to each other just five feet away from them on the other side of the hedge.

"Well, I never," Cynthia said with sudden energy.

"Come along, sister," Roland commanded. "Don't pine."

Oh, God, Kate thought, I'm going to laugh. I swear I'm going to laugh.

Hal's lips descended to her breast as she began consciously to hold the laugh in—a disastrous move. His tongue found her nipple and glanced across it as his hand started to pull at the zipper on her slacks. Kate's face was getting red; a waterfall of giggles was gathering inside her for explosion. Hal rose from her breast and saw her predicament on her face.

"They're probably down by the gate already," said Nancy Lee, her voice now close to Roland's and Cynthia's.

But Cynthia said, and Kate pictured her stamping her foot, "I don't believe that for one minute. They're in this garden somewhere."

Hal was catching Kate's giggles. He put a hand over his mouth to choke them back. When that proved useless, he buried his mouth in her breasts. But the little pants of laughter he was trying to suppress beat at her soft flesh like tiny gusts of wind, exciting her even as they increased her sense of the ridiculous.

"Come on, let's head back, sister," Kate heard Roland say again.

"How are you feeling?" Nancy Lee asked someone.

"Why, just fine," Roland responded somewhat testily.

"I mean," Nancy Lee went on, "that looked like quite a little punch you took back there."

"Just a tap," Roland huffed. "Just in fun."

Hearing this, Kate thought she would suffocate if she couldn't laugh out loud. The muscles of her stomach and along her ribs burned. She looked at

Hal; he had abandoned her breasts and was sitting up, doubled over, his face red, his hands gripping the grass.

God, which one of us is going to break first? Kate wondered in an agony of suppressed merriment. Hal looked up, his eyes giddy with pleasure.

Nancy Lee had said something Kate missed, but now Roland was answering a question.

"Just a lovers' tiff, Nancy Lee," he said.

"I just thought you seemed a little short of wind," Nancy Lee said sweetly.

Hal was beginning to pant. Cynthia's voice, complaining, was fading down the path.

"Don't you worry none about Roland," Cynthia said. "Kate'll be sorry she embarrassed us—you take my word for that."

As their voices faded Kate's eyes locked disastrously with Hal's. Simultaneously they broke into laughter, talking in whispers, all that they dared till they were sure they were out of earshot. They grabbed at each other in the ecstasy of release, falling back on the ground, burying their faces in the fallen blossoms and in each other's shoulders, holding their sides, gasping.

"Oh, I haven't laughed this way in years," Kate said in a breathless rush.

"*What* are we laughing at?"

"I don't know—everything."

Very faintly Kate heard Cynthia's shrill voice say, "Did you hear something, Roland?"

Then Nancy Lee's unequivocal reply: "*I* didn't hear anything. Come along."

Kate lay back on the ground, spreading her arms, smiling happily up into the sun. Hal's face moved into view, his eyes crinkled with happiness. He pressed an arm under her, easing her toward him, his face slick from their laughter. She closed her eyes. His lips found her neck and skimmed along it, brushing her skin, nibbling at her playfully, lovingly.

"Look at me," he whispered.

She opened her eyes. His face was above hers, one hand on his cheek, his body propped on an elbow. He was gazing down at her. She felt a spiral uncurling inside her, expressive, inchoate. From its center, she reached out for him, but he would not come close. His hands tugged at her slacks, dipped inside gently.

"No, I want you to look at me. And I want to see you . . . Rest, rest . . . no words . . . no separations."

For an instant she worried that they would be discovered, that they would miss the jitney, miss the boat later . . . She wanted to look away, not share their tumbling intimacy so boldly. But his eyes held her as solidly and tenderly as they had the night before. Soon all extraneous concerns fell away from her and she gave herself over to the languid, loving caresses that moistened her and moved her.

He was a strong, demanding lover without losing any of his sweetness. There was no such thing as a shortage of time or an urgency of need. His need, it seemed to her, was just there; it would not falter, overwhelm, or evaporate, therefore there was no reason to hurry. But as a delicious, shimmery tremor seized her body, she shut her eyes involuntarily, the image of him propped on his elbow shining on her eyelids in negative.

Soon it became her need that must be answered urgently.

"Oh, please . . ." she moaned, pulling him toward her.

She opened her eyes. He was smiling softly. Very slowly he moved over her, holding himself above her on both arms. She closed her eyes again, feeling his knees next to her thighs as she opened her legs. She grasped his hips and pressed him into her, then opened her eyes to see him close momentarily in an exquisite pleasure.

"Lie still for a moment, my love," he murmured.

She did, but could not long stay motionless. She felt in the grip of monumental forces, and she must respond to them.

"I cannot," she said, smiling up at him, a little hopelessly, as though her body were out of control.

Hal nodded peacefully, then put one arm under her shoulders to bring her close to him. "Then fly . . ." he whispered.

And she did.

The paddle wheel kicked away from St. Francisville, leaving a foamy wake as the huge boat moved magnificently upstream.

It was sundown. In high spirits, Kate dressed for the evening, picking out a green dress and a white crocheted stole. She checked and rechecked her face in the mirror, marveling at her high color and what she thought must be a new sparkle in her eyes. Flashes of their afternoon returned to her all through her dressing—the carpet of crushed lilies and violets where they had lain; the brightness of the sun through a corner of hanging moss; the slow, even sleepy desire in his eyes and the way he cradled her in one arm as her sensations climaxed. She had actually fallen asleep and they had had to call a cab from the mansion to drive them back to town. But neither had cared, and Hal had not seemed in the least concerned. It was as though they had crossed to some shore where nothing was different as much as it was better, broader, sweeter. Yet something had changed, she knew. Even though no words had passed between them, they had struck a secret bargain. She could feel it, and it had altered them in a subtle way.

Kate stepped into the lounge after dinner and saw Andy and Hal near the bar with their heads together. Some instinct told her there was trouble. It was not that they were talking together—what could be more natural?—but it was the serious, tense way they conversed, almost huddled inward. She saw Hal stick his jaw out in an uncharacteristic way, a way she had not noticed before, and then saw Andy withdraw a little from the motion, raising his shoulders deprecatingly, as though to say, Who knows? Who cares?

Though she felt Hal had seen her come in, he didn't look in her direction, and when Hitch asked her, with an old-fashioned charm, to dance about five minutes later, she accepted absentmindedly, still disturbingly drawn to the two men in deep conversation. Hitch wheeled her right by their corner, but Hal pretended not to see her, though Andy raised a tentative hand in greeting.

Alarmed and confused, Kate decided to beard the lion in his den. When the dance was finished, she went straight to the gaming table, where Hal was just dealing out a new hand.

"May I play a hand, too?" she asked, attempting a conversational tone, but sounding, she thought, tight with tension.

Hal did not raise his head but said only, "If you like," and waved to an empty chair.

Through five hands of draw poker she desperately tried to reestablish the connection she knew they had had a few hours ago when they returned to the boat. But some delicate cord of communication between them had been cut. The image of his face above hers in the garden became the more poignant as the game drew on and no sign of connection came from him. Kate searched for explanations.

Perhaps Andy had warned Hal that his interest in Kate had been noted; perhaps they had actually been seen in the garden. Though Hal was close enough for her to see the flash of his dark eyes, his manner continued to be so distant that she knew she had to leave. It was too hard to see him this way—after their lunatic laughter and delicious intimacy in the Rosedown gardens.

At the end of the next hand she rose from the table, mumbling an excuse. She was halfway across the room when she turned suddenly. Hal was looking at her, an expression of sadness and bewilderment on his face.

Kate awoke early the next morning and had breakfast alone in her room. The boat was to cruise all day, with a few stops scheduled. She gathered her thoughts together. How could she get some time alone with Hal?

In the lonely hours of the night Kate had decided that Andy had relayed her questions about Hal to him, and that Hal now felt she had been spying on him. The more she thought about it, the more she became convinced this must be the cause of Hal's remoteness.

She'd done one late-morning tour of the boat with Nancy Lee, and she'd tried to be pleasant as the perky woman reminisced about her own visits to San Francisco. But Kate was obsessed with Hal. She was not one to let misunderstandings fester, and her desire to repair the breach between them grew stronger as the hours passed. Nancy Lee finally went off to play shuffleboard with Hitch. Kate stood on the sun deck, looking at the rolling sugarcane fields giving way to stubby pine forests. The weather, she noted, mirrored her feelings, for the day was cloudy, the air oppressive.

Staring out at the swollen river, Kate began to mistrust the afternoon she'd spent with Hal and all the feelings it had engendered within her. The skiff routine, as she now thought of it, became in her mind something he'd done before, not a unique experience they had shared. As she let herself dwell on such depressing thoughts a lethargy stole over her; she sat listlessly in a deck chair, staring at the shore slipping past, or retired to her room to lounge on her bed with a book. She hoped every doubt she had was untrue. But without the ability to act—she could not possibly go down to his quarters and confront him—her enforced waiting only generated more doubts.

Finally, after a day of anguish, she bumped into him in a crowded passageway on her way to dinner. "*Hal*," she cried. "Could I speak with you a moment?"

He stopped and turned. "I'm due downstairs," he said rather curtly.

"It will only take a moment," Kate replied, trying

to keep her voice bright. He motioned her out on deck.

"I didn't want you to misunderstand my converstaion with Andy, if that's what's making you . . . a little cool. Did he say something to you?"

"I'm not cool. But I am busy."

"But—did he?" she pressed.

"Yes, as a matter of fact." Hal, who had seemed eager to get away, now came to rest. His face softened, and he leaned against the railing. "Kate," he began, looking at her sharply, "if you want to know anything about me, why don't you ask me?"

"Of course, you're right. And I apologize. But Andy and I were walking together, and you were the only person we both have in common, so it seemed natural to talk about you," she said. Her words sounded inadequate even to her. She glanced up and caught his eyes upon her. Quickly he looked away. "I *am* curious about you. I don't think that's unnatural, and I am an attorney, and I'm used to facts, not guesses. It's my instinct to keep things clear, which is why, I suppose, I feel so . . . so blown out of the water now. But I didn't mean to pry."

"Blown out of the water, huh?" he said distantly, looking over the river.

"Hal, don't you know what I mean?" She touched his sleeve. "I really care about you. Was I wrong about *your* feelings?"

"I've got plenty of feelings and they aren't really clear where you're concerned right now. Maybe we should back off a bit."

Shocked, Kate could only nod, and after a long look, he turned and left. She watched him go into the passageway that would take him to the lounge, where she knew Roland and Cynthia were waiting to play cards.

Her appetite vanished and she turned to lean against the rail. His words echoed in her mind. In retrospect, she realized they had not been spoken harshly. He had looked more sad than angry. Nevertheless, his words had hurt.

Somewhere above her, the pilot had turned on the huge searchlight, looking for a place to tie up. She watched the beam of light play across the shoreline, then settle. The boat veered toward shore. A moment later she heard the roustabout scramble down the gangway to tie the boat off with a thick mooring line. The light went off, and the boat stilled.

But Kate didn't have the energy to leave the rail. The night settled around her. She couldn't believe that Hal—who had been so gentle and had seemed to have such a fine understanding of people—would take a little incident like her conversation with Andy and blow it out of proportion. It just didn't seem like him. But, she had to admit, she hadn't known him very long. Her thoughts chased each other erratically. She agreed with him that she should not have given Andy the third degree—if that's what he'd felt it was. Perhaps it had been her manner, rather than the questions, that had set the conversation out of the ordinary for Andy.

Kate sighed deeply. Was she just going to stand here and stew? she asked herself. She pushed back from the rail and made her way to the lounge, where the lights were bright, the band loud, the dancing spirited. The gigantic paddle wheel rose above the room stilled for the night. In some curious way she was beginning to regard it as a symbol of their churning feelings for each other.

Nancy Lee sat at a little table near the alcove, where a game was in progress. Kate went over to her.

"Okay if I sit here with you?" she asked, indicating the chair next to Nancy Lee.

"Why, sure. I was just wondering what had happened to you today," the sprightly woman said. She nodded to the table. "They're into a hot poker game. Pot's big."

Kate looked at the table. A mound of chips commanded the center, but most of the players, except for Roland, had only a few chips left in front of them. Hal looked up, saw her, nodded, looked away. Cynthia sat next to Hal, Hitch next to her, then Roland, and beside him a lean black woman of about forty, Mrs. Nelson.

"Why aren't you playing?" Nancy Lee asked.

"I'm too tired to even think of betting on anything right now. Besides, my luck's down," Kate said.

"All that loping around in the boxwoods can exhaust a body," Nancy Lee remarked with a little dig of her elbow in Kate's ribs.

Kate smiled a bit sadly, nodded, and glanced back at the game. Roland sat at an angle to her, his left side exposed, and Mrs. Nelson leaned more toward Hal, away from Roland.

Kate was about to turn back to Nancy Lee when she saw Roland cleverly palm a card from the ones he'd drawn. She blinked in astonishment, then saw that he had a handkerchief in his hand, on its way up, ostensibly, to pat his mouth.

"How extraordinary," Kate muttered to Nancy Lee. "Did you see that?"

"What?"

"Roland palmed a card," she whispered.

Nancy Lee drew back. "You must be mistaken."

"No, I'm not."

Nancy Lee eyed her carefully. "You don't look like a drinker to me." She laughed, but her laugh held a note of doubt, too. "Are you serious?"

"Yes," Kate said emphatically.

A chair scraped back suddenly, and Roland was on his feet.

"That's cheating. I *saw* you," Roland hissed loudly. He was looking at Hal. Everyone was caught by surprise.

"*Roland,*" cried Cynthia. Hitch looked furious and embarrassed.

Mrs. Nelson rose. "What are you saying?" she questioned, aghast.

"That he's cheating," Roland said, quite red in the face. Everyone was dismayed. In the main room the band played loudly.

Hal remained calm. "You're mistaken, Roland. Here—count the discards."

"I don't need to. You discarded two and switched another for your third card."

Hitch said, "Roland, what the hell are you doing?"

"I tell you, he's switching cards on us."

"What for? We're not playing for big money here."

Nancy Lee surveyed the situation, then glanced at Kate. "I'm going for the purser," she said.

The group at the table took no notice.

Kate knew better than to rush into the fray right away. She was confident of what she'd seen, but she didn't want to make a scene unless it was necessary. She decided to let the group settle down a little and try to sort it out among themselves. If they could not, she would help.

"Roland," Hal was saying, still calm and well mannered, "I can't imagine what you thought you saw, but I certainly wasn't switching cards. Did any of you notice how many I discarded?"

"Three," Hitch said promptly. Cynthia said she hadn't been counting, but Mrs. Nelson agreed with Hitch.

"That's not the point," yelled Roland.

"How many did I draw?" Hal continued.

"Three," said Hitch and Mrs. Nelson in unison.

"He drew two, and he took a third from his pocket," Roland insisted. He turned and for the first time saw Kate sitting behind and to one side of him. She met his gaze evenly. It seemed to galvanize Roland into more elaborate accusations.

"There are people, you know," he said, first to Kate and then to the table of players, "who just can't stop themselves. It doesn't matter that there's no real money on this table."

Exasperated, Hal sighed and leaned back in his chair. "Everyone put your cards on the table facedown. And keep them there."

The group did as he asked except Roland, who complained about it. But at that moment the purser arrived, and Roland's cards went down on the table. Roland immediately launched into his story, embellishing it this time with crude insults. Kate saw that he was a little drunk as he aggressively restated his charges.

"Anybody else see anything?" asked the purser,

who was apparently considering Roland's accusation seriously.

"Bob, I—" Hal began.

"Just a moment," the purser said sharply to Hal.

Kate was about to speak when Roland interrupted.

"This guy," he said, jerking his thumb at Hal, "has done it before, but I didn't want to say anything because my sister's a little sweet on—"

"Damn it," Hal said, rising from his chair at the same time Cynthia shot to her feet, crying, *"Roland."*

"Everybody calm down and sit down," said the purser. "Game's over."

Though she couldn't imagine why Roland was being so incredibly stupid and abrasive, Kate knew she would now have to embarrass him publicly.

"Ah, purser," she began, forgetting the man's name.

"Bob Talmadge," the purser said, turning to her.

"I saw everything."

Hal was looking at her now, his eyes boring into her, his face pale. But he didn't move an inch or make any sign indicating he felt she was going to implicate him.

"What did you see?"

"I was sitting here with Nancy Lee. First, I think it would be helpful if everyone sat down as he was so you can see exactly what took place."

"Very lawyerlike," muttered Hitch with a smile as he sat down.

"Nancy Lee?" said Kate, indicating the woman's chair. Mrs. Nelson sat down in her place, then Cynthia, who was shooting looks of pure fury at Roland. Hal gave Kate another hard look, then pulled out his chair and sat. Roland was last, but he seemed suddenly pleased and turned around to smile at Kate.

"Like this?" asked Roland. His smile was not lost on Hal, but again it drew no panic from him.

"Yes. Mrs. Nelson, you were turned more toward Hal, since you were picking up the replacement cards he'd just dealt. And Hal"—she faced him and felt her heart pound; his coolness was admirable—"you were turned a little more to your left."

"Wait a minute," said the purser. "How come you remember all this?"

"She's a lawyer," Nancy Lee piped up. "I expect they're trained to observe."

"Okay," the purser said, "go on, Ms. Perry Mason." He smiled, trying to lighten the situation, but no one felt very light.

"I had sat down here a few minutes before and I was trying to get a sense of where they all were in the game, who was ahead, and so on," Kate said. The purser nodded. "Which is one of the reasons I was watching the game closely instead of talking to Nancy Lee." Kate glanced at all of them at the table to make sure their places and attitudes matched the picture in her memory. "Roland, you were turned this way a bit, away from Hitch."

"Like this?" he asked again.

"Hal," she began, noting a flicker in his eyes that she could not decipher, "you were asking for replacements when I sat down." Hal kept his eyes unfalteringly upon her; Roland sighed politely, as though this recital were something to be humored. "Mrs. Nelson, you'd just gotten your cards when I saw you, Roland"—Kate picked up his hand of cards—"take one card in your left hand."

"What?" he exclaimed.

But Kate, smiling a little, lifted her finger to admonish him. "Now, where would you put that card I saw you take?" She tried to keep her voice light.

"*Wait* a minute *I* didn't take any cards from my hand," he shouted.

"Hold it," cried the purser. Roland shut his mouth grudgingly. He was turning beet red.

"Let me get this straight," the purser said to Kate. "You saw Mr. Dupuis take a card he shouldn't have taken?"

"That's right. He'd been given his replacements, had put them in his hand, and looked at them. The next moment, he had a handkerchief in his hand. He'd put the card he'd taken from his hand, the one he didn't want, into the handkerchief."

Everyone stared at Roland except Hal, whose gaze remained locked on Kate. She moved slightly toward Roland.

"Now, where would you put that card you palmed, and where would you keep its replacement? It had to be someplace where you could reach it easily." Again Kate smiled sweetly at Roland. Then deftly and quickly she plunged her fingers into his top jacket pocket—his handkerchief pocket. As he twisted away from her she drew out the card—the three of clubs.

"Roland," Cynthia gasped, "I have never been so humiliated in all my life." She was close to tears.

"Now I've seen everything," Mrs. Nelson snapped. "A grown man doing something like that in a game that was strictly for fun."

"Okay, okay. It was all a joke to see if Hal was on his toes and could keep his cool under fire. Just a joke." Roland was flustered and flailed around in his explanation clumsily.

"Of course," Hal said. "Things were getting a little dull." He eyed the pot in the center of the table pointedly. Kate saw the purser look at Hal with admiration. "Well, the game's over now. Why don't we draw for the winning pot between Mrs. Nelson, Hitch, and Cynthia. Is that agreeable?" he went on smoothly.

It was. Hitch won the draw, and the purser called for a round of drinks on the house. Kate turned to face the main room. It was amazing that almost no one out there had realized what had been going on in the alcove, she thought. But, then, the attention of most of the passengers was still on a Country Western singer who was just wrapping up his set to happy applause.

"What a horrible incident," exclaimed Nancy Lee. "I was wondering when you were going to get into it."

"I didn't want to embarrass Roland if I could help it," Kate said.

"What if you hadn't found the card?"

"Then it would have been my word against his," Kate said brightly.

"Ah," said Nancy Lee, rolling her dark eyes. "I see you're used to this. Courtrooms?"

Kate nodded as they squeezed by the tables toward the bar.

Kate had just received a glass of wine when she saw Hal come back into the room and stand about twenty feet away at the end of the bar, facing her.

"Why do you think Roland did that?" asked Nancy Lee, picking up her drink.

"I haven't the faintest idea," Kate responded, looking at Hal as he ran a hand through his red hair and accepted a cup of coffee from the bartender.

"I am so sorry all this happened."

Cynthia had come up beside Kate and Nancy Lee. "I'll have a brandy Alexander, please," she said to the bartender. "It was very silly of Roland," Cynthia went on as Kate and Nancy Lee turned to her, "and it probably wouldn't have happened if you hadn't been so rude to him yesterday." She looked pointedly at Kate. "If you don't mind my saying so," she added. The bartender gave her her drink. "More than that, the oil business hasn't been that good recently and he's mighty concerned about his work. Of course, you wouldn't have known that, but it is a factor, I'm sure."

Kate thought her apology and explanation for her brother transparent and flimsy rationalizations. Neither endeared Cynthia to Kate or, she suspected, to Nancy Lee, who was gazing out over the room with an affected, cool indifference. Kate felt sorry for Cynthia in a way; though delicately pretty, she didn't seem to get much fun out of life. Kate had the feeling that though she was smart, Cynthia meddled in things just to stir them up, just to break the boredom or loneliness of her life.

"But I'm sorry Roland let his drink get to him tonight. I hope you won't judge my brother too harshly." Her blue eyes regarded Kate through her glasses, and her lashes fluttered just a little. Kate could see a young, endearing quality in the woman, even if it was a trifle insincere.

"Of course not," Kate said.

"We haven't had much time to chat," Cynthia said, obviously trying to make conversation. She tilted her fine-boned face toward Kate and smiled. "You must have a fascinating career."

"Oh, no more than you do in a bank, I imagine," Kate replied.

"Have you had any cases that involve banks?"

"One. Age discrimination against a woman. A firm that owns banks in California and in the South—Kentucky, Tennessee, and Florida."

"Oh, that sounds really interesting," Cynthia said, looking out over the room briefly. Then she turned back. "I'm a loan officer in New Orleans."

Kate didn't quite know what to say, so she smiled and sipped her wine. Cynthia left shortly afterward, saying she wanted to check on Roland before she turned in.

Kate turned and caught sight of Hal again. He was still at the end of the bar, and as their eyes met he tipped his coffee cup to her in a salute.

Chapter Six

❦

Kate didn't know if it had been the faint rustle or a slight movement she saw out of the corner of her eye that alerted her. But now a slip of folded paper lay just inside the door to her room. She put down her book and climbed out of bed to retrieve it.

"It read: "Would you let me in, please? Hal."

Kate cracked the door to see Hal standing there in his gambler outfit, open longing on his face.

"What's going on?" Kate hissed through the door. But Hal only raised his eyebrows as though to ask again, May I come in? She opened the door fully.

"How did you know I was still awake?" she asked when he was inside. She closed the door.

"I didn't." He stood, his feet slightly apart, a half smile on his face.

"I might not have seen the note until tomorrow morning."

"That's true. Then I would have had to stand outside all those hours." His eyes glanced off her face to a place on the wall behind her. "Kate, I . . ." He took a step toward her. "I want to be with you in this room more than with anyone anywhere else in the world. I was impetuous—if you know me longer, you'll see that I'm that way by nature—but I'm sorry I distressed you."

As she listened to his rather stilted but emotionally charged words, she became aware of how shallow her breathing had become. Hal took another step toward her.

"You're a knowing kind of woman. I'm lucky to have found you." His eyes bored into her as he raised his arms and let them slip around her. Then he put one hand behind her head, palm open, keeping the other at her waist to draw her gently toward him.

She came to him haltingly, desperately relieved yet ambivalent about his apology. "You are a mercurial man of the first order," she breathed. "But I am so happy to see you."

Hal's eyes closed for a moment as though he'd been delivered from his last doubts. His arm around her waist tightened. "I am absolutely smitten by you," he whispered. "The only explanation I can offer for my rash reaction was that I care about you." Kate opened her mouth to interrupt but he placed a finger over her lips. "And caring about you as I do, it jarred me the more to hear from Andy that all you could do was ask questions about me. Andy is protective of me. He knows the precarious life I lead. He's seen other women's curiosity about me on these cruises and knows how difficult such situations can become."

"Do you like your job because it provides you with chances for fresh relationships?" Kate asked as calmly and unemotionally as she could. She wanted a straight, honest answer.

"That is not at all what I expect or want from this job." He looked at her boldly, one hand now on her shoulder. "What happens between you and me is our business, and I can assure you that it has never happened like this before. Never."

Kate could feel all her defenses dropping as her vulnerability to him crept in through the door of her affection for him. She welcomed it. She put her cheek against his shoulder and felt a quiver of anticipation shake her.

"But I *am* impetuous," he murmured, his warm breath stirring her hair. "And I'm all hyped up about the derby, and I'm not as calm as I may appear to be. And part of that, putting aside the derby, is your fault." He laughed lightly. "I think of you all the time, and I don't want you to be away from me for a moment." He tucked a hand under her chin so she would look at him. "Thank you for not storming around the boat looking for me today. I needed some time alone, and it would not have been appreciated by the powers that be."

"But if you win the derby, you won't have to work on the boat, will you?" She smiled.

"That, madam, is true. And I look forward to that day."

Only inches away from his face, she looked up at him in silence. Her lips longed now to cover every corner of his body. She took his hand and led him to the bed, pulling down the rumpled covers. Then she turned out the light. Dimly, through the windows, the reflected lights of the boat shimmered on the tree-lined shore.

Kate slipped out of her robe, lay down beside him, and propped herself on her elbow, loosening the buttons of his shirt.

"You're undressing me, lady. Have you lost your

senses?" Hal teased, succumbing happily to her deft fingers.

"Yes," she said, "I have."

She opened his shirt slowly, kissing his chest, then pressing against him so that he could feel the soft fullness of her breasts through the sheer material of her gown. She heard him groan faintly, then he wrapped his arms tightly around her.

For what seemed like a long time, they lay together on the bed, feeling the wonder and relief of closeness after separation. Kate's hand found the clasp of his trousers.

"I'll do that," he whispered hoarsely, rising.

She watched him undress, silhouetted against the windows, his motions long and smooth and quiet. When he returned to her, folding her into his arms, the branding of their earlier lovemaking came back to her with force. The tangy smell of him invaded her senses. She looked into his eyes in the darkened room and felt a surge of warmth for him inside her.

Gently, slowly, one of his hands came up as his lips swept her face. And she felt, in the darkness, that he "saw" her as completely as anyone ever had before. The thought of such intimacy once would have scared her; even now, with Hal, she had to force herself to meet it without flight. Yet, when she met it, it seemed more right than anything that had ever happened to her.

His hand closed around her hair and pushed a lock back from her brow. "I am so glad to be here with you," he murmured. "Tell me what you feel."

She felt clogged by her intense emotions and practically unable to speak. "I . . . don't know," she finally said. "I feel so awash in my emotions . . . I'm just getting reacquainted with them." She leaned back a little. "I love being with you," she said even more softly, "and being known by you."

"What do you mean, being known by me?" he asked.

"I have the feeling that sometimes, when you're looking at me, you see me completely, not just the good part or the public part, but the private and secret sides. And that you accept them—all of them—without judging. Does that make sense?"

Hal nodded in the darkened room. "I guess so."

"It's a great gift you give."

"What gift?"

"That pretense or acting isn't needed. I don't have to be nice all the time or fake feelings, but just be myself."

"I like you—just the way you are."

She reached to stroke his lean, muscular shoulder.

"But it's scary, too. Because I know you won't be satisfied with anything less than absolute honesty."

"But you are honest, aren't you?"

"Yes, I am." She brushed her lips against his shoulder.

"Then, why is it scary?" he asked, stroking her hair again.

"Because it takes practice to be so aware of your feelings and then to express them with someone else, not hiding them or shading them. I . . . I'm beginning to feel that I've never really allowed myself to just *be* with a man." She kissed him softly and felt his thighs move against hers. "Hal, you inspire a kind of open love that I've . . . just never felt before."

"That's because I care about you," he murmured,

drawing his hand down her ribs and putting his palm against her breast.

"No, it's more than that. It's a quality in you that will not settle for less than the whole person." She flung her head back in frustration. "God, I'm not making any sense."

"Yes, you are." He gripped the back of her head and raised her lips to his, his tongue searching her mouth delicately. When at last he released her, she drew breath in sharply. His lips found her breast as his fingers combed away the gown gently, and she ceased to be aware of her gasps for air as her mounting desire seized her. She lifted her head to taste his cool, full lips again with all the passion that was reawakened in her.

A soft groan escaped him, and his breath warmed her neck as he kissed her over and over again. He pulled at the thin straps of her gown, easing it down to her waist, then he raised her up in his arms, his mouth and tongue on her nipples drawing a moan from her. She felt him pulling the gown away slowly and when it was gone, she crushed her body against the length of his, her mouth fastened on his.

"I know you," he said, "I know you." He was trembling, his hands now on either side of her waist as he entered her tenderly. She arched against him, feeling the joy of their reunion. Then he slowed and put his head on her shoulder.

She stirred. "I want you so desperately," she heard herself admit. "You fill my senses even if I just see you across a room." She gasped as a river of emotion ran its course through her. He had begun to stir again, increments of tiny movements like the flick of a tongue or the faintest breeze on a vine. His kisses came more slowly and languorously, hanging sweetly on her lips and breasts. And then she saw him raise his head to look down at her, his eyes glinting in the reflected light and shadows. His arm slipped under her, raising her still higher in the ecstasy of their bonding. Propelled by a force building within her, she leaned into him, her breasts against his chest, and kissed his lips, drawing them into her mouth, releasing them, drawing them in again. The sensation started shock waves of pleasure in them both that were so acute she finally broke away, felt her head going back, meeting his hand flying to support her neck, felt him plunge deeper into her, felt herself collapsing inwardly, her bones melting as he caught and held her in their descent.

She did not know how much time had passed before she heard him talking to her. How long had he been talking?

"I understood tonight why you're a good lawyer." His words were so low, his tone so in keeping with their lovemaking, and his lips so close to her ear as they lay together quietly on the bed that she was not at all surprised he would choose this moment to say them.

In the same tone he went on as though he expected no reply. "You didn't just spring into the situation—you picked your moment. I liked that. And the way you strung us along—you lulled Roland into feeling so secure that the accusation completely unnerved him." He nuzzled her gently and pulled her tightly into his arms. "I'm glad you're on my side." He laughed softly, holding her close.

* * *

The next morning, long after Hal had reluctantly left her, Kate drank coffee on her veranda, watching the flat, lush land slip by. The boat had outrun the clouds of the previous day, and the morning promised fair and sunny weather. She warmed the cup in her hands and let the verdant land lull her.

I'm falling in love with him, she said to herself, incredulously. I can feel it rising in me. I would risk myself for him. Would he for me? What does he feel, under that charming exterior?

Over and over again, as the big boat glided upriver, she kept thinking of him, of his wonderful eyes, his bold yet gentle gaze, his full, animated mouth, the confident yet sensual walk, the facile, loving, tender hands.

Suddenly she sat up straight in the white chair and put her cup down. Was she—could she be—falling in love with the *image* of a riverboat gambler instead of the man himself? She groaned audibly. This wonderful boat trip provided an artificial atmosphere that was all freedom and no debts, all play and no responsibilities. It was nothing like real life. Relationships formed on it would probably never survive. And at that thought, tears rose in her eyes.

As Kate looked back on it later, she knew that she had never been happier than on that day in Natchez. The sunlight was warmer and brighter; the trees greener, sporting their new spring leaves; the flowers more deliciously scented; the people in Natchez the friendliest in the world. Or so it seemed, because she saw it all through the rosy gauze wrapping of her love. When Hal's hand touched hers or when she reached an arm about his waist, she thought she had never felt a touch as sweet. And when they moved apart, she was instantly lonely. But she had only to turn and fill her eyes with his image, watch the angular, handsome face move as he talked, to be content again. It was amazing, she kept thinking, how important a person could become in such a short span of time. He had stepped into her life and filled a void she had not even been aware existed. As long as she lived, she knew she would remember this day as absolutely perfect.

They walked into town like carefree tourists with Nancy Lee, Hitch, and Andy, and all the while Kate stole glances at Hal. Under the pretext of speaking with their new friends or scanning the town, she mentally undressed him—right there on Broadway Street. She saw again his slim, naked hips, lithe waist, high, small buttocks, and long, lean legs covered with a downy red hair. In her vision, his muscular arms coiled around her and his lips brushed her temple invitingly.

"Let's go to Natchez Under the Hill," said Nancy Lee, "and hear some good jazz."

"It's not even noon yet. Let's save the music for later," said Hitch.

"Okay," Nancy Lee responded cheerfully, "what about going to the Rosalie mansion and then some lunch—huh, Kate?"

Kate smiled and nodded, completely engrossed in her fantasy. In her imagination, she was looking down into his face as she was slowly sinking to his chest, nuzzling her nose into the corner of his neck.

"What do *you* say, Hal?" Kate tossed at him softly. He was leaning against a wrought-iron railing, his smile warming his face. The edges of his lips raised a little higher.

Hitch and Nancy Lee and Andy were debating in which direction Rosalie lay. Hal pushed himself off the railing and drew close to Kate.

"I know what you're thinking," he whispered. "You're undressing me in public." His voice was so soft she wasn't sure if she'd heard him correctly. But just under his words she could hear the pleasure he was taking in them.

She whispered back, "Do they know?"

"Everyone knows. Everyone." He took her arm and moved her slightly away from the little group, then stepped away from her, ostensibly to look out at the river. He leaned his hands against the railing as her eye followed the line of his body. Suddenly he turned, took her hand, and pulled her over to him. "Now you," he said. He placed her with her back to the railing and stepped away from her. His dark eyes and amused mouth caught the sun for a moment as the wind tossed the branches of a tree. His eyes were like fingers, and she could feel them seducing her, revealing her.

"How much does everyone know?" she whispered.

"I will bet you that these three know everything there is to know, lady."

"What are you two whispering about over there?" Hitch called out. "Come on—Rosalie awaits."

Hal squeezed her hand secretly, digging her knuckles into his thigh. They broke apart.

"Don't you want to see Rosalie?" asked Nancy Lee, coming up to them.

Andy laughed. "Yes, Hal, don't you want to see Rosalie?"

"I go where you all go and gladly." He took Kate's arm gaily and swung her into Broadway Street, and the others followed.

They walked south, parallel to the river. Kate felt it had become their steady companion on all these magical days.

"I think I'll break off here and look for you at Connolly's," said Andy as they reached the parsonage. Everyone agreed that Connolly's would be the perfect place for lunch, and the company parted good-naturedly, but Kate thought that she saw Andy give Hal a pointed look as he turned east.

"Think of the money it took to maintain a house like this," Hal said as they wound their way through the white Tuscan pillars on the portico of the Rosalie mansion.

"Think of how hard the life was for the women and the slaves," Kate countered. "Houses like these weren't kept up with a lot of electric devices but with labor—l-a-b-o-r."

The tall windows of each gallery wore wooden shutters and the rosewood furniture gleamed.

"Why, women were kept on a pedestal," Hal argued, stopping by a display of Sèvres china in a glass case.

"First of all, most women weren't on a pedestal, and second," Kate said, ticking her points off on her fingers playfully, "the few who *were* lived lives of boredom and virtual imprisonment. It was an idyllic life only for wealthy white men."

Hal peered at her. "You don't like the South, do you?"

"It's not that, Hal. It's just that I think we ought to be aware of where reality stops in history and myth takes over."

He turned and took her hand, creating that instant intimacy that did not invade privacy but expanded the link between them.

"Then it's lucky we live in the twentieth century, isn't it? I would never wish to see you trapped."

She heard Nancy Lee and Hitch approaching and did not want this moment with him broken. As he had done before, he seemed to read her thoughts, and he pulled her around the edge of a tapestry screen, then took her in his arms and kissed her. His hands lingered at her waist, his fingers gently kneading the skin through her clothes. Hal seemed to have neither timidity nor taboos, yet his caresses held no hint of violence or plays for power.

"What do you want most?" he whispered, his mouth against her ear.

"At this moment?"

"Yes."

"For this day not to end." She clasped the back of his head with her hand and kissed him deeply. Then she clung to him, pressing her body as tightly to his as possible. She wanted fervently to be a part of him and he of her, no matter how brief their time together would ultimately be.

When they left Rosalie, Kate turned back for a moment. A vine of yellow roses clambered along the brick wall of the house on the near side, its leaves fluttering slightly in the warm breeze. Kate knew that she would always remember his kiss and his question at Rosalie, that the moment there had been singled out, imbued with a unique flavor. She turned. Hal was staring at her quietly, and she felt he shared her thoughts.

As a body, the four of them walked up Canal

Street to the house on Endicott Hill: Connolly's Tavern. A plaque at the door announced that the tavern was originally the terminus of the Natchez Trace, the road from Natchez to Nashville, which had been carved out of the wilderness in the 1780s and functioned as a thoroughfare until the 1830s.

She looked up. It was a large house with two stories, and nine slender columns in front stretched between the two levels of galleries. The tall French windows looked out over the Mississippi.

"I'm starved," said Kate as they entered. "Let's eat a bushel of catfish."

"Don't you ever stop eating?" asked Hal. "It's a wonder you aren't as big as this house." He put a friendly arm around her shoulders and picked a candy out of a dish by the desk. "Here, this will hold you."

"Not for long, chum."

To Kate's delight the tavern had a real brick floor, high, vaulted ceilings, and meters of carved wood.

"It's so comforting to look at," Kate said as they joked about her fascination with the decor. They sat by a window overlooking the river.

"See?" Nancy Lee winked at Hal. "She'll never get over it."

"I hope not," Hal said quietly. Under the table he put a hand lightly on her knee.

They stuffed themselves on crawfish and catfish, hush puppies and cornbread sticks, squash casserole and sweet potato pie and beer. And they laughed when Hal started telling tales of the river. He turned out to be a fine raconteur, delivering punchlines with faultless timing, and he had a laugh that could set anyone else laughing, too. Kate couldn't figure out quite what it was—maybe the pitch of his voice, maybe the way the laughter tumbled out of him in waves. But whatever it was, Hal's laugh catapulted Kate into instant mirth.

Gradually, as they sat at the table long after lunch, Kate realized—for the first time—that she and Hal were being perceived as a couple. When a remark was directed to her, Hal was included; when she asked a question, sometimes Hal would augment it. It was a good feeling. And even under Andy's watchful eyes, Hal did not hide gestures of gentleness—a light touch on her wrist, the alacrity with which he filled her coffee cup, or, earlier, when he had pressed her to taste the crawfish he held out just after it had arrived steaming from the kitchen.

They ended the day at dusk, watching the sunset from the flat-decorated bandstand in Bluff Park, two hundred feet above the river. Low on the horizon, the sun threw streamers of red and yellow and orange light on the water. The five of them sat on a bench and stared into the glow, buried in thought. Hal stood, after a moment, and leaned against one of the delicate pillars, looking out at the water, a serious yet contented cast to his face. Kate, warmed by his closeness throughout the day, began to feel the dread of parting from him. No matter how rare this delicious and impetuous infection that had invaded her, she knew it must end in a few days. The thought filled her with melancholy but their parting was as inevitable as the departure of the sinking sun.

Chapter Seven

❧

Kate sat in a deck chair high above the paddle wheel, watching hills of rolling, foamy water spread out in the wake of the boat. The flat, green land they passed with a measured progress toward Vicksburg came straight down to the edge of the river; in places it was hard to see where land ended and river began.

Neither Kate nor Hal had been able to let the other go after they'd returned to the boat from Natchez. He had stopped by her table at dinner, chatting with the group but looking only at her; she had gone straight into the lounge afterward, where she'd watched him perform card trick after card trick for the amusement of the crowd, his deft hands producing cards and coins from nowhere. And later, in the still night, those same hands had curled around her waist and breast, his sensuous lips leaving no part of her body unburned or unloved.

A blast from the calliope, whose pipes rose above her, jarred her out of these reveries. A calliope contest was beginning and she turned to see the pretty Cynthia, a little overdressed, take a stab at the huge device. She was cheered by a small crowd of contestants and observers, but she played with astonishing gusto. The sweet, shrill music spilled out like an invisible foam in their wake.

"She's good."

Kate turned to see Hal standing behind her chair.

"Yes, she is at that," she agreed. Their eyes met and silently acknowledged the night before. Cynthia's song rolled forward energetically.

Kate felt as though she were smiling with all her muscles, each one turned up at the edges, until Hal bent close to her and said, "Our relationship has been noticed—unfavorably." Kate questioned him with her eyes. "The captain remarked this morning that my favoritism is not welcome."

"How much trouble are you in, Hal?" she asked, a frown of worry etched into her forehead.

"Quite a bit," he said cheerfully. "But nothing that can't be dealt with." Behind the chair, hidden from the eyes of the group around the calliope, he squeezed her hand. "I don't care."

She could tell that he did care. "You're just saying that. Are they going to fire you?"

"Not yet."

"You mean if you aren't seen with me anymore, or if we don't get caught or if—"

"So many ifs." He smiled.

"What are you going to do?"

"What are *we* going to do?" he asked, staring away from her and lifting his head as though he had already decided but did not want to say yet.

A searing pain went through Kate at the thought of not seeing him for the rest of the journey, but she was ready to suggest it when Cynthia finished her rendition of "Old Man River" with a resounding finale. She hopped off the bench and made her way through light applause to them.

"Are you enjoying the trip so far?" Hal asked her, flashing a smile.

She nodded. "Most of it," she said, letting her long eyes, under her glasses, linger on him.

"You sure played up a storm on that old calliope," he complimented her.

"Why, thank you, sir," she said, bobbing a curtsy. But Kate saw that when Cynthia glanced back at them, she had a cool, almost cold look on her face. "You two certainly have your heads together down here. You look like conspirators." She giggled lightly. "Anyway, we're getting up a little party to go into Vicksburg," she went on, looking at Hal. Her voice sheathed a challenge in the invitation. "I don't suppose you have the time to come with us."

"Mademoiselle," he said, bowing a little, "nothing could please me more."

Cynthia smiled but it did not warm her face much. "Why, how delightful." She turned to Kate. "Isn't that nice?"

"Yes, it is," Kate said. Cynthia waited a moment for Kate to say something else, but Kate only stared back at her until Cynthia, disconcerted, returned to the calliope contest.

"She didn't invite you," Hal said.

"Oh, never mind. I'll go in with Nancy Lee. I want to get postcards and some other things, and being seen with a whole new group might take the heat off you."

"Do you always think of everything?" he asked, smiling.

"Nope. I have blank spots sometimes." She smiled back at him.

*   *   *

Kate stood outside a little store in the center of Vicksburg, peering at a rack of postcards. She had picked out a collection of Southern mansions, some views of the river, and was reaching for a magnolia tree in bloom when, through the empty slots on the rack, she saw Hal's face peering at her mischievously.

"Oh," she gasped in surprise, and nearly dropped all her cards. He chuckled and moved out from behind the rack.

"Let's go over to the park. I want to talk with you," he said urgently.

"But what about—you'll be in trouble—" Beyond him she saw the same group he'd left the boat with, Cynthia among them, disappearing around the corner.

"Don't worry about them." He laughed. "I've made another choice."

"Cynthis will be very ticked off."

"She'll get over it." He took her hand. "I want to talk with you."

The National Military Park, commemorating the forty-seven-day siege of Vicksburg during the Civil War, was a great deal different from what Kate had imagined. It was a huge park, covering many acres where the remains of Confederate trenches and the remnants of breastworks pocketed the lush land. They were the only indication of the fierce battle that had been fought.

They sat down on a stone wall by a grove of trees and looked out at the rifle pits and gun emplacements.

"I suppose you're going back to San Francisco from St. Louis," he said after a moment.

"I left that open," she said, watching a lark on a branch nearby. "I have a month off. Having planned everything in my life, I thought I wouldn't plan this." She smiled at him.

"Come to Kentucky with me," he said, watching her face carefully.

It was the last thing she had expected him to say, the one contingency she hadn't planned for, and she knew her shock must be plain on her face.

Breaking into her surprise, Hal took her hand. "Don't answer right away. Let's walk, Kate."

"Come to . . . Kentucky?" she finally asked, hesitantly.

"Let's walk."

They moved into the shelter of the woods, skirting little beds of wild flowers.

"You mean . . . for the derby?" she questioned, trying to understand what the invitation meant. Hal stopped walking and pulled her into his arms.

"No, I mean . . . I love you, Kate. I love you."

Taken utterly by surprise, Kate could think of a thousand things to say, and none. His cheek was pressed to hers as he said, "Yesterday, when we were on the bandstand, watching the sun go down, I felt so unbearably lonely, knowing that in a few days you would be gone, that life would go on, and you wouldn't be with me. I want you with me, Kate. I love you."

He stepped back, holding her by both shoulders, a quizzical smile brushing his lips. "What are you going to do about it?"

She shivered. The woods were aglow with lush greenery and the smell of damp spring soil. "I—I don't know what to do," she stammered. The birds suddenly sounded very loud from the heights of the trees.

"Come. Come here." He pulled her down by a little hillock of moss that might once have been a crater carved by Union cannonballs. But now it was soft and green—a perfect, private bed for lovers far away from the park's tourist traffic.

"Hal," Kate said, "I'm just . . . I'm not saing no— but I was preparing myself not to see you again."

"I was, too," he mumbled. "But then today, as I was walking with Cynthia, I realized that I don't want you to go out of my life. How do you feel?"

"I feel . . ." She sought for a key to her mixed emotions. "Confused."

"Is that all?"

"No," she said, and then, with more force, "Oh, *no*." She reached out for him and he took her in his arms. "Oh, Hal, I do love you, it's just that . . ." She was reeling.

"Shh," he said, then kissed her deeply, pressing the small of her back with one hand as though to weld her body to his. It was a delicious, tantalizing, powerful kiss. As his hand moved slowly and with exquisite tenderness into her blouse, nuzzling her breasts, she leaned back onto the moss, his body following hers. Kate ached with desire for him; a flame ignited each time they met.

She groaned, "Oh, Hal, I don't know what we're going to do—"

"Come with me, Kate. I love you."

"Oh, I don't want to leave. It's not that, Hal."

She was yielding to him without the slightest remorse or hesitancy, gazing up at the tender and special man that some cosmic accident had placed in her path, feeling the slip of clothes against flesh, the firm coolness of the ground under her, the warmth of his touch.

"You know that I know you as no one else has," he said. "We recognized each other the first moment we set eyes on each other . . ."

She felt him run his hand along the tender inner skin of her bare legs until he reached her panties. Pushing aside the thin silken barrier, he stroked the very core of her as his lips brushed her cheek all the way down to her neck. She raised her hips and moaned, then reached out for him with both hands to lead his pleasure-giving touch even deeper inside her. The tiniest whisper of a motion from him sent spasms of pleasure rippling through her, fanning the engulfing flame of her desire for him. Yet, even in the cocoon of her blazing senses, she could hear that cooler part of her say, he can't mean this. It's in the moment of passion . . . Another tendril of sensual pleasure reached out of her as his tongue left a trail of delight along her breast. She longed for all his words to be true, yet distrusted them in a way she couldn't possibly explain. Nothing in his face or voice asked her to say anything in response.

"Don't move," he whispered. "Let me look at you."

She lay still, the leafy, spatulate branches swaying above her in a dreamy slow motion. "I adore you," she breathed.

He raised his head, his eyes sweeping her face. "It's more than that. I am in love with you, Kate, and whether you know it or not, you are in love with me." Suddenly she knew it was true. "We can't pretend."

With a swift motion, he took her in his arms, lifting her from the ground at the waist, at the same time rising to his knees, bringing her head against his shoulder while he still caressed her deeply inside. Then, as suddenly, he broke their union, and with a strength she didn't know he had, he brought her to her feet and leaned her against the sheltering tree, then put both hands on either side of her. Her blouse open, her skirt at her feet, he entered her.

"I am the equal of you, Kate," he said softly but decisively, "and I shall have you." She was impaled, her sensations soaring as she clung to him. She arched her back and let the fire consume her as he bent over her, embedding himself deeply within her. His legs were stretched far apart, his knees pressed against the outer edge of hers. His lean hips tilted forward, he covered her with his chest and loins, spreading a moist warmth through her with every gentle stroke.

"I know you," he whispered hoarsely, "I know you as I know myself. I know right now what you are feeling. I know how to make you feel even more. I know you can make me feel as no other. We belong together, Kate."

His slow, passionate movements sent her sailing into a canyon of sweet pleasure. She could not stop her hips from moving, and as she reached up for him, both his hands gripped her around the waist.

Dizzy with the sensations he created within her, she knew the sounds she heard, muffled by the damp, deep woods, were hers alone—yet they seemed not to be coming from her body. His hand cupped the back of her neck as the sweet waterfall of feeling drenched her. Then she went limp and fell to her knees on the soft moss. Hal knelt beside her, hugging and rocking her. Gently he eased her down on the ground and covered her with her skirt. She gazed up at his wistfully smiling face, and he, trembling, lay down beside her.

It was more than an hour later that they began to talk again.

"We've only know each other a few days, Hal," she whispered.

"I want you to come and live with me," he said, his profile to her as he looked up into the pale green leafy trees that swayed above them.

"And I want to, Hal. I want to. But I can't just drop my law practice. People are counting on me. I'm due back in court in a few weeks."

"I want you to come and live with me. We'll work it out." He rolled over and kissed the end of her nose.

"Are you always so impetuous?" she asked.

"Always. We belong together and you know it."

But did she? she wondered, turning away to look up into the trees. How much she would like to just drop everything and run with him, as though life were the fantasy of leisure that the riverboat vacation tried to create. But this wasn't a cruise. This was reality.

She turned back to him. His eyes were closed, his sharp nose and full lips perfectly outlined against the greenery behind him.

"What do you expect from a relationship?" she asked, kissing his cheek.

"I expect you to be there when I need you and I expect to do the same," he said, not opening his eyes.

"Yes, loyalty, support," she said. "And what else do you expect?"

"I'll protect you, and you'll protect me. I'll sing to

you at night—you didn't know I could do that, did you?" She shook her head, smiling. "I expect good humor and fairness. And—" he looked at her—"I would ask for your love." They looked at each other in silence. She reached out and twined her fingers in his hair. "Now, it's true," he went on, "that I don't have a lot of money—but I will."

"Money is not the issue."

"I just wanted to put that in for the record," he said playfully.

"Hal, be serious. This is serious."

"I am serious. Never been *more* serious." He opened his eyes and turned to look at her troubled face.

Nothing sounded better to Kate at this moment than the prospect of waking up each morning and finding Hal next to her. But her cautious nature warned her that he had said nothing about marriage and nothing about permanence.

She propped herself up on her elbow. "Are you asking me to marry you?" she asked forthrightly.

"If you want to be married, yes." He was smiling.

"But what do you want?"

"Counselor, I want you—any way I can have you."

The words and the tone had a charm that brought an unbidden smile to her lips. Why was she holding back so much? she wondered. What had he not asked her that she wanted? She turned her final question over and over in her mind, trying to find ways of saying it without saying it. At last she knew she'd just have to spit it out.

"Why must I be the one to change my life around to suit yours? Why can't you race your horse in California?"

"Why, I intend to race her all over." He laughed.

"Well, stable her there, then."

"That's a lot easier said than done," he groaned, rising up on both elbows. "It's not just moving a horse, but her stablemate, finding a new trainer and stables, insurance—and how about my little patch of land in Kentucky?"

"Well, it's not easy to move a law practice, either. There are commitments to meet, exams to pass for another license when you move to a different state." As though from a great distance, Kate felt the panic rising inside her as she heard herself pile objection upon objection. It was as though she stood outside herself and she was powerless to stop. Finally, Hal put a hand over her mouth.

"You're afraid," he said, looking at her with his incredibly soft and searching eyes, the eyes that seemed to know everything.

"Yes, I am. And if you had any sense, you would be, too." He shook his head sadly. "We're such different people. How do we know we're not just caught up in a web of romance? This is all so . . . crazy."

Moving to his knees, he put both hands around her face. "It is not crazy. Your head's leading your heart. Listen to your *heart*," he whispered forcefully, his voice shaking.

It was an accusation she had heard before. Yet, even seeing his anguish and feeling her own, she could not bring herself to say yes. She thought of so many other things she could say: I can go with you for the derby. We can spend the week together— even two . . . And she looked up at him and saw a kaleidoscope of unspoken thoughts on his face, too. They were both hemmed in by their different lives and commitments, and she knew he could no more suddenly uproot himself from Kentucky at this moment than she could from California. He dropped his hands. She was so deeply enmeshed in her thoughts, thrilled and troubled at the same time, that she had not felt him rise.

"Don't you have anything to say now—you who always have so many words for everything?"

"Oh, Hal, please don't be angry. I've got a lot to say, but I need a little time."

"If you had a lot to say, you would have said it, Kate. All you can think of are objections. And *think* is certainly the word for you. Don't you *feel* anything?"

"I do. I feel thrilled and upset and happy and sad and overwhelmed . . . and confused."

He made a dismissive gesture with one hand, and she could clearly see the pain in his eyes. He stood over her, biting his lip. "Could it be," he asked softly, "that you feel a man who raises a horse and comes from a farm just isn't quite the sort of man you want?"

She looked up at him, astonished, letting his cool, soft words sink in. "No," she said unhesitatingly.

He studied her. "Well, think about it."

"The point is, Hal, that I can't just abandon my work and responsibilities in a moment. What kind of person would I be if I did that? Please try to understand."

He tossed his jacket over his arm. "I *am* trying to understand." He started away from her.

"Hal, don't leave like this," she cried.

He did not answer, just kept walking across the battlefield, skirting a gun emplacement, heading toward the boat. She watched him with mounting exasperation and loneliness, feeling besieged herself, until her eyes blurred and she felt the hot tears spill down her cheeks. She knew he was terribly hurt, but she did not know how to repair the damage of the battle they'd just endured.

Chapter Eight

When she got back to the boat, Kate went straight to her stateroom, and the instant she shut the door behind her, she burst into tears.

She lay on her bed, letting the tides of her argument with Hal wash over her, and finally fell into a restless sleep.

Kate saw him walking across the deck of the boat with that conspicuous rhythm all his own. As he came toward her she felt again the inner pleasure at the half smile on his lips, the roll of his shoulders, and the bright patch his red hair made under the sunlight. Nearing her, she saw his dark, warm eyes.

A wing of delight rose in her, and she anticipated his loosely possessive embrace—but he walked straight past her.

She turned to hide her confusion and looked out at the muddy river. The Mississippi changed, as she stared at it, into a roiling lake. The breakers pushed against the boat, rocking it dangerously. She hung on as deck chairs began to slide and passengers screamed. She couldn't find Hal anywhere. She was running through the obstacle course that had become the deck, over chairs and purses and life jackets and a saxophone, when the huge white boat turned on its side and capsized. As she hit the freezing water, she woke up.

It was night. She looked at the clock after a moment's disorientation. After nine. She'd missed dinner.

Just as well, she thought. I wouldn't know what to say to anyone, and I look a mess. She glanced again in the mirror to confirm this and was contemplating going back to bed when she thought, This isn't an ordeal—it's a vacation. She quickly got out of her rumpled blouse and skirt, and plunged into the shower.

When she emerged from her stateroom, she wore a long cotton skirt, a ruffled blouse, heels, and drop earrings, and she felt much better. She made her way up a flight of stairs and down the long corridor to the lounge.

"There you are," cried Nancy Lee, who stood just inside the door. Hitch was at her side. "We were looking around for a table, and we had just decided we'd have to go up on the balcony." She pointed to the ledge of tables above the floor. "What kind of day did you have?"

Kate parried, for she hated to lie, no matter how small the issue at stake. "Very pleasant for part of it. What did you do in Vicksburg?"

Nancy Lee's round, kind face took on a sudden sprightliness as she dove into a description of her day's activities. But Kate saw that the woman also regarded her astutely.

"You certainly are decked out," Hitch said. Then, changing the subject, "Look at that Cynthia." He jerked his head toward the alcove off the lounge. "She sure can pour it on when she wants to."

Kate saw Cynthia was energetically shuffling a deck of cards at a table of bridge next to the poker table. She had on her evening glasses, which were fancier than the daytime ones, and was wearing a bouffant blouse with puffy sleeves. But it was the sight of Hal that warmed her and chilled her at the same time.

He was in his tuxedo and ruffled shirt, whisking cards around the table to the assembled players. The agony of their afternoon returned to her full force, and a spear of sadness and regret invaded her. She gripped her little bag, suddenly seeing her dressy clothes as a pathetic, unsuccessful attempt to deny all that had happened between them that day.

Hal looked up as he put the deck of cards aside and saw her. The crowded, noisy room receded, and only the force of their locked gaze seemed real. But the set, closed expression on his face did not change one iota. He broke the connection between them by glancing down at the cards in his hand, then across the tables to Cynthia, who, Kate now realized, sat facing Hal from her place at bridge.

In dismay, Kate turned away and saw that the entire exchange had been witnessed by Nancy Lee. The little band struck up "Summertime" just as Hitch found a table for them above the crowd at the edge of the upper level.

Seated, Kate could look down not only on the entertainment below, but, if she turned her head a little to the right, she could see Hal and half his table.

"What'll you have?" asked Hitch jovially.

"A brandy," Kate said without thinking.

"Oh—into the hard stuff, huh?"

It was difficult to get served, the place was so

jammed. Finally, Hitch got up and went down to the bar. When he was gone, Nancy Lee leaned close to Kate.

"You ever raise orchids?" she asked.

"No," Kate responded, bewildered by the question. "Did you?"

"Yes. Once. These cruises sometimes exaggerate reality, and a friendship takes on the quality of a hothouse flower."

Nancy Lee was offering her ear for a gentle confidence, Kate knew, but Kate was not up to it. It was hard enough to sort out her own feelings, let alone give voice to them in this Babylon of music and talk and song. Instead, Kate smiled at Nancy Lee in a way that she hoped would thank her for her offer, then turned her attention to the singer. He was prancing back and forth on the small stage, holding the mike as close to his mouth as he could without actually swallowing it. But in a moment, Kate realized, she was comparing the way he moved to the way Hal moved. Hitch returned with their drinks and a funny story about Roland, who'd become ill at dinner and had had to go back to his stateroom.

"He's allergic to onions," Hitch shouted, "and there were onions in the—" Kate couldn't hear the last word.

"In the what?"

"In the *SOUP*."

"What's funny about that?"

"The scene he made, as though someone had set out deliberately to poison his last days on the boat."

In a rush, his remark brought home to Kate again

that her time here, in Nancy Lee's "hothouse," was
limited and transitory. It would end all too soon, and
she was not ready for that finality.

The following morning, Kate felt no better and the
day itself did not help. A gray bank of clouds came
up early, pressing a lid down upon the river. It made
the warm air soupy and humid. The threatening
weather did nothing to improve her state of mind—or
heart. She went up to the sun deck—a misnomer this
day—and plunged into the pool. The water and exercise felt good. She swam lap after lap, consciously
trying to exhaust herself, to push away thoughts of
Hal and erase her own doubts about him. Had Hal
been right? Could her reluctance possibly be due in
part to snobbery? The idea seemed absurd, yet his
accusation disturbed her, and she examined herself.
But she could find no trace of embarrassment about
his chosen interests or his origins. She liked that
difference in him very much. What gave her pain
now was her own conservative reticence, her inability
to reach out and take what was offered and hang the
costs or criticism. She swam another grueling lap in
the pool, blowing the water away from her face. Was
it wrong to feel responsible? It seemed to her now
that Hal thought so. Had she fallen in love with
someone who truly didn't understand her need to
have her own career? Yet, dangling in front of her,
she could hear the underside of his words. She turned
on her back and floated. It was as though he had
said, Be brave. Follow your heart. We can work it
out—if we want to badly enough. Be impetuous—it's
okay to be impetuous a few times . . . Never, she

reminded herself as she gazed at the leaden sky, had he said, Give up your silly practice.

Had she been inflexible and blind? She rolled over and swam ferociously, but no amount of exertion would dissolve the profound concerns she felt emerging within her. Finally, she climbed out of the pool, panting, toweled herself off, flopped into a deck chair, and tried to forget her worries and nap.

She went down to lunch late and picked her way through the remains of the buffet, having little more than a salad and cold shrimp, which was all she wanted anyway. She was seated alone at the far end of the room, near a bank of windows, when she saw Hal poke his head inside and look around the room. But he did not appear to see her and was gone a moment later. His appearance broke Kate's concentration, and what little appetite she'd managed to muster disappeared. She felt a wave of despair sweep over her. Rising hastily from the table, she marched briskly across the room and out into the corridor, hoping to catch him. But he had disappeared.

Returning to the almost deserted dining room, she ordered a coffee and sat back to look at the river as the boat took the center channel. She was practically alone, except for a few latecomers. The stewards were carrying the big platters of cold meats and cheeses and fruits back to the kitchen. The soft clink of china drafted over the room.

Outwardly, Kate knew, she seemed calm, but inside, she was in a turmoil. Hal's declaration—if that was what it was—consumed her. It was not that she didn't have the time to go to the derby with him before she returned to San Francisco; she could have said yes to that, she reproached herself now. But at the bottom

of it all, she was still amazed and taken aback by his
assumption that of the two of them, she should be the
one to make all the changes. It was not possible for
her to put down and pick up her work to satisfy
whims or passions—was it? And if they were talking
about life—changing decisions, then that would be
an even more difficult decision, certainly not one
made in a moment. Perhaps, she feared now, Hal
had little respect for her work or for her commitment to it, which was every bit as strong as his for his
filly. As she watched the stewards rearrange the table next to her, she considered Hal's respect for her.
She shook herself out her obsessive thoughts. No,
the root of her doubt came from something else. As
the day wore on, through kite flying and attempts at
reading and even dinner, she began to come to the
conclusion that she was at fault for not telling him
enough of her life, how hard it had been for her,
too, to work her way through college and law school,
and what an abiding passion she had for her career.

The next morning they would stop briefly at Cairo,
and the day after that, they would dock in St. Louis.
The trip was all but over, and it made Hal's distance
from her that evening the more painful. Almost
unable to tolerate the noise and frivolity in the lounge,
as well as his coolness, she still remained a while just
to watch him—his curly red hair glinting under the
lights, his angular, handsome face half hidden in
shadow. And she wondered, as she watched him, if
she had made a critical mistake on the Vicksburg
battlefield, one she would forever regret.

She watched him rise from the table when Andy
appeared in the lounge and saw them talking in a
corner; Andy was gesturing energetically, excited

about something. Hal looked sharply in her direction, shaking his head in a kind of sad bewilderment. Then both men turned away, and she somehow knew that there was no way to reach him that night.

A knock at the door the next morning brought Kate awake suddenly.

It was Nancy Lee standing in the hallway, wearing a gray jogging outfit, a hood pulled over her head. She was running in place.

"Thought you'd like to have coffee and rolls with me on my veranda," Nancy Lee said.

Her room was on the river side of the boat, which meant that they looked west as she and Nancy settled down to steaming coffee with sweet cream, and butter and hot bread.

"Why are we stopping at Cairo?" asked Kate as she reached for a roll.

"Don't know. Unusual but I'm sure nothing's wrong. Even though it's a pleasure cruise, there's still the trace of the attitude that steamboats are still transport, and if they're asked to pick up something or take something off, they do it." Slowly Nancy Lee reached out and began buttering a roll.

"You've got a problem," she said.

"I've got a problem," Kate agreed, looking out at the river.

They talked for an hour, and Kate found herself confiding practically everything to Nancy Lee. The boat had stopped and started again during their exchange, sliding away from land into the river with a slow and careful majesty that Kate found thrilling.

"Now, I don't know much about Hal Lewis," Nancy Lee was saying, "But I do know he's honest and decent and smart. But he's never met anyone quite like you before—and you sure as hell haven't met a man like him."

"What do you mean?"

"I mean," Nancy Lee said with just a hint of the professor in her voice, "that you have to look at the totality of your life. Hal Lewis wouldn't ask you to join him without a lot of feeling behind it, and though he's a gambler in a lot of ways, he isn't a fool. He probably wants to find a way to spend time with you off this hothouse boat to see if you two really get along."

"He certainly didn't say anything like that."

"He said he was in love with you. The big question, which you haven't even approached, is, are you in love with him?"

Nancy Lee's quiet words hit Kate like a blow. It was true—she had not dealt with her own feelings, she had not allowed them any air at all, and as she sat back to let Nancy Lee's words sink in, Kate was amazed at the depth of her emotions. She realized at that moment, that, no matter how great the coincidence, she had by sheer chance met someone who respected her, challenged her, and loved her, by his own startling admission, and it really would not have mattered if they had met on this boat or on a plane or at a party. The point was—they had met.

Nancy Lee buttered another roll and put a dollop of honey on it. "This is so sinful," she said, raising the roll, "it's wonderful." She bit into it slowly. Kate sipped her coffee; it was cold.

"If people want to work things out—*both* people, that is—they usually find a way to do just that." Nancy Lee smiled as she polished off her roll.

Kate rose and kissed Nancy Lee on the cheek. "You are a very special friend and I hope I know you for many years to come."

Kate left Nancy Lee's stateroom feeling better than she had in many days—more like her old self. She was not ready to change her whole life around for Hal, nor impetuously to declare unending love and commitment, but she was ready to open herself to his love and to see what time would bring them.

But how to find Hal now? She'd never been to his quarters and she knew he had no set place during the day where she'd be sure to catch up with him. She decided to go to the purser; she could say she left an earring on the gaming table last night.

The purser was in his office tacking up a copy of the daily schedule on the wall, but he wasn't much help.

"Hal? Something came up for him and he had to leave the boat this morning at Cairo. Captain's pretty hot about it. No more cards."

His news left Kate nearly speechless with shock, but she managed to conceal the input his words had on her and to escape gracefully. Unable to think what else to do, she headed back to Nancy Lee's stateroom.

"It's nothing to do with you," Nancy Lee assured her after Kate delivered the news, "but just to check, I'll go see Andy. He's a friend and I'm sure Hal wouldn't have left without telling him why."

"He probably couldn't have left without getting Andy's permission anyway," Kate said bitterly.

It was noon. Doubts and remorse assailed her. She couldn't imagine why he'd left the boat unless some grave emergency with his filly had arisen, yet she felt that was not the reason. If it had been, he would have told her, she was sure of it. Why had she not told him last night that she had to talk with him? Would he have refused? She didn't think so.

Now that she was more aware of her own feelings, she saw there were so many things she could have done differently, so many things she'd left unsaid. Kate paced the room, then strode out to the veranda, recalling their first evening—no, it had been dawn when they'd brought coffee back from the galley. The water had been light gray with a sheen of dawn cast on it like a glaze, and the shore had slowly disengaged itself from the night, a tree here, a house there. And over the hill, she remembered, the pinkening sky had limned the ridge. She remembered his downcast eyes as he held the coffee cup, and the moment he'd looked up questioningly at a comment she'd made—quiet, self-assured, he'd been, courteous, yet full of humor and goodwill. Now he was gone, and deep inside Kate blamed herself.

Nonsense, she thought, pacing back into the room. He left because he wanted to or needed to.

She looked around the room and felt a prisoner there as much as she was of her own thoughts. Unable to endure the lack of activity, Kate left the room and headed forward to the purser's office. No sign of Nancy Lee. She walked back to the stairs, went up two flights to the observation deck, and there, as she was about to turn and check back toward the stern, she found Nancy Lee and Andy, accompanied by Hitch.

"We were just coming down," said Hitch. Behind him stood a rather morose-looking Andy.

"Why don't we go up top?" suggested Nancy Lee. In silence, they made their way to a top deck at the rear of the boat, where tables and chairs were set out. A short, uncomfortable silence ensued as they all sat down.

"I was very distressed to hear that Hal Lewis had to leave the boat," Kate finally said. "I hope nothing happened to his horse."

"Not yet," said Andy, looking at her sharply. "What kind of law do you practice, Miss Sewell?"

"Oh, please call me Kate," she said quickly. It was clear that his loyalty was to Hal, and he was no friend of hers.

"Public law," she answered. "My clients are the elderly who are having difficulty getting work or housing, some employment cases, battered wives and children—that sort of law."

"You work with banks?" His steely eyes pinned her.

"Nope. Not unless they've fired someone without cause or just before they were to collect a pension— cases like that." Kate ached to get to the bottom of his questions, but she knew he would do it in his own time and that it would further antagonize him if she tried to press him.

Andy turned to Nancy Lee. "I guess maybe you're right, but I wouldn't have given you the time of day if you hadn't been on this boat so often," Andy said.

"Of course I'm right," Nancy Lee declared.

"But I did what *I* thought was right and I'm not sorry." His sharp eyes glanced back at Kate without a shadow of apology.

"What is everyone talking about?" asked Kate.

Hitch leaned back in his chair, his arms folded over his chest as though to ward off an assailant.

Nancy Lee looked at Andy challengingly, and Andy looked down at the river.

"Do I get three guesses?" Kate persisted.

Andy tilted forward in his chair and raised his eyes from the river. "Hal left the boat because he thought there was some trouble brewing about his filly."

"Oh, dear," said Kate, "I just knew something was wrong. Please tell me how I can help."

"Don't think you can. He thought you were the trouble."

"I?" Kate exclaimed, puzzled.

"Best start at the beginning," Nancy Lee said.

"Yup. Guess so," he said, and turned to Kate. "You see, Cynthia Dupuis came to me and said she'd learned that one of your clients—is that the right term?"

"Yes, if you mean someone who has come to me for advice as a lawyer."

"Guess so. That one of 'em is a Kentucky bank."

"So?"

"Do you have dealings with a Kentucky bank?" he shot at her.

"No, not exactly. I do have a case pending against a banking group for age discrimination. One of the banks in the group is in Kentucky. But the bank isn't my client—the women who are bringing the suit against it are."

Andy seemed to weigh her words, then said, "Hal's taken out a big loan from a Kentucky bank—as big as he could get on that little sliver of land. He also had to use the filly as collateral." Andy kneaded his long, bony fingers together. "I mentioned to him what Miss Dupuis told me. Looks like she had it wrong, but you know Miss Dupuis is in banking and both he and I thought she'd know what she was talking about. Anyway, the news kinda rattled him. He was afraid the bank, which hasn't been too friendly of late, was going to move in and collect his filly for nonpayment. 'Course, that was the first time I'd heard that he hadn't been able to make his payments to the bank."

"The man overreacted," Nancy Lee suggested.

"Now here, here," Andy put in, "he's put everything into his filly and it ain't been easy, and when he saw a direct threat so close to the derby—which she stands a good chance of winning—he *moved*. Any one of us would have done the same."

He reached into his pocket and pulled out his wallet.

"But, but," Kate stammered, still trying to sort it all out, "did Hal think I was on the boat for any other reason than, well, pure chance? Is that what you're saying?"

Andy was pulling a carefully folded newspaper clipping from his wallet. He handed it to her. "This ran in the Lexington papers just a couple of weeks ago. There's been a lot of press down our way about Hal and his filly. He's one of a kind."

Kate unfolded the paper. A large photo showed Hal standing next to a long, lean thoroughbred. The headline read: FARMER GAMBLES ALL ON FILLY.

"I still don't understand."

"He thought you were in the pay of the bank."

"In the pay of the *bank*? How incredible," she exclaimed indignantly.

"Well, hired by the bank, I should say. They're about to force him to file for bankruptcy, and he's already heard from one lawyer about what'll happen if he doesn't pay up pronto. But I thought he'd settled the matter until after the derby. Guess not."

"But doesn't a horse have to win a certain amount of money in purses to be eligible for the derby?" asked Kate.

"Sure," Andy replied. "But Hal owed a lot of money before she ever won anything. I'm sure whatever she's won has gone right into paying those debts. Then there's insurance—that's real steep these days—and travel expenses. Mounts up pretty high."

Kate looked from Andy to Hitch to Nancy Lee.

"How could he believe I'd do anything to . . . that's just *awful*. Why, he must have thought . . . No, I just can't believe it." She felt light-headed as the full impact of how her ambivalence toward him in the park might have struck him, how he might have interpreted it. Then she thought of her conversation with Cynthia the night of the disastrous card game. "Wait a minute. Cynthia did know we had a case that involved a Kentucky bank. She really must have mis-understood what I was saying."

"Well, we were just kinda talking," Andy said. "It wasn't as if she deliberately came along to deliver a message or anything."

"Some people are just plain mean," said Nancy Lee. "I think Cynthia took a shot without thinking much about it—and just happened to hit the bull's eye."

"Horse, in this case," muttered Hitch.

Kate remembered the night she and Hal had spent in the bayou, how she'd seen Cynthia on the boat deck when they had returned at dawn. She wondered if Cynthia, deep down, was jealous, too. "Isn't this a mess?" Kate said quietly.

A steward came up to them to give Andy a message.

"I'll be right there," he said. Rising, he put a hand on Kate's shoulder. "I'm real sorry if I caused any misunderstanding. But you must know that Hal comes first with me, and I was duty bound to tell him what I'd heard."

Kate stood. "Of course, Andy. I'm sorry it turned out this way, but it's not your fault. And I'll see if I can't fix it, too."

Andy regarded her carefully. "I told Hal I didn't think you threw that kind of punch. You got spirit."

"Where's Hal now?"

"Flying back to the stables where his horse is training."

"Would you give me the address?"

"You bet," Andy said. "You can get a plane out of St. Louis, if that's what you want. But I warn you— Hal's not in a friendly mood. You'll probably have to do a lot of fast talking to get him turned around."

"You just watch me," Kate said.

When Andy had left, she sat down again with Nancy Lee and Hitch.

"If I'd seen a movie," Kate declared, "I'd never have believed it possible that Hal could do this."

"Real life beats everything," said Hitch. "What are you going to do?"

But Kate was still trying to take it all in. "How could he have done it?"

"Oh, I can see it, sort of," Nancy said. "When anyone's struggled against all odds the way I think Hal has, and when he sees the chance of a lifetime within reach—his filly winning the derby—and I guess that's a real possibility . . ." Nancy Lee fluttered the clipping. "Well, that person would move real fast and ask questions later."

"Yes," Kate said, looking at Nancy Lee knowingly, "and I never came right out and told him how I felt. How could I have been so . . ."

"Hold it." Nancy raised her hand. "There is nothing written that you have to know at all times how you feel and then put it into words."

Kate looked at her with affection and put a hand on her arm. "You are priceless," she said gently. "You really are."

"I'll second that," Hitch said quietly, kissing Nancy Lee's cheek. And Kate, seeing the depth of their affection for each other, realized again what she had lost.

The huge boat churned on toward St. Louis and made no further stops. Kate couldn't wait to get off it now, but since there was no hope of that, she would settle for a few words with Cynthia.

Dinner the last night was formal—or as close as the informal trip achieved—and an air of celebration hung around the ship. But to Kate the boat was empty without Hal. She looked out at the dark shore; no white and glowing ibis there now, she thought, standing by the rail. For her the boat had an abandoned air and she couldn't shake the feeling.

She had to confront Cynthia just to make sure she had indeed said what Andy had reported. Andy was stubborn and loyal; he was no liar. But Kate knew she would never feel right about the matter if she didn't talk to Cynthia.

When Cynthia excused herself to go to the powder

room, Kate followed. When she entered, she found Cynthia applying lipstick.

"I'd like to have a word with you, Cynthia," Kate said.

"Sure." Cynthia glanced at her, then back into the mirror. Quickly, without accusation, Kate told her what Andy had said and about Hal's departure.

"Yes, I heard he'd left," Cynthia replied, "but I don't think I ever said any such thing to Andy."

Kate could feel her impatience begin to stir, so in order not to lose sight of her objective and to take her mind off it, she began to observe Cynthia closely. The hand holding the lipstick was shaking.

"Don't you remember? I told you that a Kentucky bank was in the group of banks I had a case against?"

"Well, I guess you did say something like that one time." Cynthia was still concentrating on getting the lipstick on straight. "I may have mentioned something of the kind. What difference does it make?"

Kate realized suddenly that Cynthia's banking experience would give her access to information about loans that many people wouldn't have. She could certainly have been very credible to Andy.

"I think it caused a misunderstanding," Kate said.

Cynthia jammed the cap on the lipstick brush. "If it did, I'm sorry," she said without remorse.

"I certainly have no claims on Hal, but I did care about him and—"

"Now, now, are you in a lather, Kate?" Cynthia interrupted, a false smile widening on her face. "It all seems to be a silly misunderstanding."

"That's not what I thought, but I wanted to be sure," Kate said. For a moment Cynthia frowned, then she grabbed the door handle and was on her way out before Kate realized it. "Cynthia, wait."

She caught up with her in the passageway. "I know you probably didn't know what Hal's reaction would be—"

"Frankly, Kate," Cynthia said, drawing herself up, "I would never be interested in a man like Hal Lewis." She lifted her pale eyebrows. "After all, honey, he only works on this boat and was paid to keep company with the passengers."

The insult surprised Kate. "I'm sorry you feel that way, Cynthia," she whispered.

Suddenly Cynthia's face collapsed. "Oh, I didn't mean it the way it sounded, really I didn't." Her hands fluttered. "I *had* counted on spending time with him. He's handsome and nice. It was obvious he preferred you. But really, I never meant to say anything out of line."

Kate felt drained. "No, I can see that. I'm glad we talked."

"Andy seemed so . . . interested that I just ran on and on, I guess. I'm sorry."

"I am too, Cynthia," Kate said wearily, and without another word, Cynthia hurried away.

Kate leaned against the railing and felt the clammy breath of the river. She wanted to be off that boat and in Hal's arms desperately. She would fly directly to Lexington, and as for the ultimate outcome of her meeting with him, Kate made no predictions. It would be as it would be.

Chapter Nine

༈

The world of stables and racetracks was alien but instantly exciting to Kate. She smelled leather at first, worn leather, then fur, and dirt, straw, and wood. It was only after cataloguing these scents that she became aware of a horse peering over its stall at her; it whinnied softly. She heard the muffled clop of horses' hooves and the rustle of their huge bodies against the walls of their sheds.

Hot and dusty from the flight, Kate stood at the entrance to the south stable. She had not changed clothes but still wore a corduroy jacket and slacks she'd put on in St. Louis that morning. At the Lexington airport she'd rented a car and driven straight out to the Sheffield Stables, where Andy had said Hal kept his horse.

Kate looked around and drew a deep breath to steady her nervous anticipation of seeing Hal. The clear, clean air was laden with the smell of fresh hay. She had not let herself plan what she or Hal might say; she only hoped that at the right time she would know enough about how she felt to describe it to him. But she could not still her excitement.

Would he greet her coldly? Would he greet her at

all, or would he find a way to evade her? How surprised would he be?

On the drive out, she had pushed such thoughts away and had concentrated on finding the right roads in the unfamiliar landscape. Rolling hills stretched as far as she could see, green and lush, broken by distinctive white fences or groves of trees. The air was sweet and still.

A woman emerged from one of the stalls and came toward her, leading a horse by its halter.

"Hello," Kate said to her, "I'm looking for Hal Lewis." The woman was lean, muscular, and short; she had cool blue eyes under the brim of her straw cowboy hat, and she looked about thirty-five years old. "My name is Kate Sewell."

Kate offered her hand, and the woman took it gravely, shifting the horse's lead to her other hand.

"Ann Sheffield," she responded curtly. "Hal's not here."

"Oh, I thought his horse was stabled here."

"It is." Ann started to walk and Kate followed. The horse was huge, and of a brown so dark it almost looked black.

"Can you tell me where he is?"

"You from the press?"

"No, just a . . . friend. I'm in town for only a few days."

"Staying for the derby?"

"Perhaps."

They broke from the stable into the sunlight. Ann stopped. "He's over there," she said, nodding toward another long, low white building. "In the paddock on the other side."

"If he's busy—"

"They're just taking pictures." Ann cast her a bleak, dry smile. "For a magazine," she added.

Kate thanked her and headed toward the building. Her heart was thudding. She had wanted to see Hal alone for this first moment; perhaps she should wait back at the stable, she thought. But she walked on, over the soft, sandy loam, and rounded the corner with more than a little trepidation.

A photographer was just entering the paddock, where two horses—a palomino and a golden-brown thoroughbred—raced each other across the paddock; they made a sudden stop, reversed themselves, then charged back to the end wall again. Of the two, it would have been easy to tell which one Lady Lydia was even if Kate had not known the color: the palomino, though pretty, was chunky and no match for the aristocratic lean brown horse. Kate saw that Lydia did have style—that inexplicable but identifiable quality whose presence set any animal or person apart.

Hal held the gate for the photographer. A wide-brimmed hat hid his red hair and shaded the angles of his face, but even from this distance his movements were unmistakable. He had not seen her yet and Kate was content in this first electric moment to leave it that way.

The two horses approached the photographer slowly craning their necks. When they reached him, they nuzzled him as though this motion would tell them what kind of cameras hung from his neck. Then the palomino playfully took off and Lydia followed at a lope, head high; for the photographer's benefit, it seemed to Kate. No matter what kind of lead the palomino had, she would be quickly outdistanced by Lydia unless, Kate suspected as she watched them, the thoroughbred allowed her stablemate to hold the lead.

As Lydia stopped abruptly, ears up, and faced them, Hal turned to the photographer and said something. The man was backing off for a shot, but the mischievous horses were onto him, following like puppies. Both men laughed as the photographer backed straight into the paddock wall.

Despite their playfulness, Kate saw that both horses were alert at all times, ready to be off and running at a sign. At one point Hal clapped his hands, and their heads jerked up in unison and they trotted off gamely.

The photographer nodded at Hal, who opened the paddock gate. Outside, they talked together a moment, then the photographer started off to the main building, waving at Hal as though to say he'd find his own way out. Hal looked after him a moment, then turned back to the horses. He leaned on the rail as they came over to him, pushing at his arm and shoulder with their muzzles. Kate started toward them.

It was Lydia who signaled Kate's nearness. She pricked up her ears and shook her head. The shorter, stockier palomino whinnied. Hal, his back to Kate, turned. A look of astonishment came over his face before it hardened into a cold mask.

"Hello, Hal," Kate said softly. Her emotions were so charged it was hard to get the words out evenly.

"Kate . . ." His deep voice rumbled—an unwelcome note in it—and the horses backed away a little. Kate looked about, uncertain how to proceed.

"Is that Lydia?"

"Yes."

Kate approached the rail. The filly eyed her.

"She's beautiful," Kate said. Lydia tossed her head and flicked her tail with disdain. Hal leaned on the rail, staring into the paddock, away from Kate.

"I had to see you," Kate began, feeling choked up and inarticulate. "We'd shared so much—"

"Too much."

His voice was so cold it sent a chill through her. He hooked a boot over the lowest rail; it tightened the leg of his jeans as he brought an arm around the fence post, hiking himself up to sit on the top rail. Kate went to the railing and leaned against it as a silence fell between them. Beside him now, and below, she was looking up at the line of his jaw and the curve of his hat brim. It was not an angle conducive to talking. She studied the railing, dropped her purse on the ground, and pulled herself up to sit beside him. She was relieved to attain the uncomfortable perch without teetering too much.

"What's a thoroughbred?" she asked.

"Just what it says. Mark of breeding, character, conformation, beauty." She could hardly hear him.

"How do you know if a horse has all that when it's still young?"

Still looking away from her and at the horses, which had cantered away, he mumbled, "Can't, really."

"But there must be some way to tell, otherwise—"

"Look to the head."

It was an awkward conversation, but as they talked, Kate noticed that the horses were working their way closer, trying not to appear interested.

"You can see a horse's courage and intelligence on its face just as you can on a person's face," he said. Kate looked at Lydia. Her head was well set on a long, fine neck that rose smoothly out of muscular sloped shoulders. Her muzzle was straight, tapering to flaring, full nostrils. Hal called to her and she came over immediately. Reaching out, he stroked the filly. "She's got good width between her eyes—means she has a good brain, some think. Look to the legs, too, of course," he added.

Lydia's long, sloping shoulders blended smoothly into lean, bony, delicate legs.

"They seem so fragile," Kate said.

"They are. When a horse reaches its top speed, it's going maybe forty miles an hour, and for an instant one leg is bearing its full weight. A half ton of horse flesh is pounding down the track supported by a section of bone and muscle only a couple of inches thick. Well, you get the picture."

"I missed you when you left the boat," she said. Hal grunted. "It was very sudden. I think there's been a misunderstanding."

"How did you find me?"

"Andy."

Hal looked at her briefly, raising his eyebrows, then turned away. "I didn't know he was a confidant of yours," he said.

"He's not. I said I wanted to clear up a misunderstanding. I told him my side of it, and he agreed."

Silence. Then, "Hal." An exercise boy of about sixteen came up to them. Hal turned.

"Ann wants to see you—"

"I know, I know." Kate saw Hal's face darken, and he looked over at the filly.

"What's wrong?" asked Kate.

"My filly's under the weather," he barked, jumping off the fence.

"She looks great to me."

"How would you know? And what are you doing here? You don't belong here."

The exercise boy retreated. Hal looked after him, then mumbled, "I've got to talk with Ann. Is there anything else?"

Kate climbed off the fence, her hands clammy on the rough wood. Hal did not offer to help, nor did she expect it.

"Yes, there's a great deal more, Hal. I came a long way and I hope you'll find an hour so we can talk."

He looked at her sharply, adjusted his hat, then nodded. "Okay." He began to turn away. "It's only that I'm concerned about Lydia."

Kate knew it was a lot more than that, but she said nothing.

"She's not rating well on the track."

"The track?"

"The schooling track here. She's just not . . . with it," he finished lamely.

She saw the creases of worry on his face clearly now. How different he looked from a few days ago on the boat, dressed as he was in jeans, jacket, and boots, his hands thrust deeply into his pockets, his hair jammed under the hat.

He walked ahead and Kate followed. Did she miss the gambler who had been replaced by this curt, no-nonsense horseman? she wondered. What they had shared on the boat was over—that much was clear—yet the memory of his tender strength lingered with her. What parts of their time together remained with him? she questioned, crossing the soft, sandy soil behind him, then pausing as he stopped to talk with Ann. Was she foolish to be here? No, she thought, she still felt the connection and she believed he felt it, too.

Ann glanced at Kate, then turned away from Hal as he called out to the exercise boy, gesturing toward Lydia.

"Maybe she's nervous, too," Ann shouted as she disappeared into the stables. Hal looked back at Kate.

"You wanted to talk?" he asked.

Kate approached him, gathering her thoughts.

"Hey, Hal," cried the exercise boy. "She goes back—that what you said?" Hal nodded, then joined the boy as they walked toward the paddock.

As the boy came abreast of them, Hal took Lydia's halter and walked away from Kate without a word. The boy followed with the palomino.

Kate looked around. She was surrounded by stable sheds and paddocks. A long, low, white houselike structure sat by the main road to the north. In a far paddock, three horses galloped and whinnied, young and exuberant.

Kate followed Hal into the stable. From nearly every stall, a horse eyed her. Hal was down at the far end.

"I can't really talk now. I guess I can listen, though," he said when she joined him.

"I know."

Lydia snorted. Hal bent over and ran his hands down her front legs. Rising, he smoothed her neck with his open palm, his expression worried and a little distracted.

"What's that?" Kate asked suddenly. She pointed at a white bird sitting calmly on a perch in a front corner of Lydia's stall.

"Cockatoo," Hal replied.

"I know it's a cockatoo, Hal. I mean what is it doing in here—in her stall?"

"Company. Lydia and Peter like each other."

"Isn't that unusual?"

"Nope, not really. Horses are herd animals—they need company."

"But cockatoos? *They're* not herd animals."

"No, but he and Lydia like each other. Can't explain it any other way. Other horses like a particular dog or cat, sometimes a goat."

"Ann told me where you were. Is she the owner?"

"Niece of. She's one of the trainers here and a damn good one, too. I trained Lydia with her." He rubbed the filly's muzzle, took a blanket off her back, and hung it on the rail. "It's wet," he said. "That's not—never mind." He replaced it with a fresh one. Kate could see he was really worried.

"Can I buy you dinner?" she asked.

Hal shook his head. "Gotta stay here tonight with Lydia. What did you want to talk about?" He leaned back against an inside wall of the stall and folded his arms against his chest. His dark eyes swept her face boldly but without warmth. "It's okay now. We won't be interrupted—day's over here."

Day was over outside, too. The sunlight was slipping away and the shadows inside the shed lengthened.

Kate felt an overpowering urge to hold him, to soothe the corners of worry that made him seem so remote. The memory of his lean, comforting body rose in her like a warming flame.

"I've missed you a lot, Hal." He snorted. "I *have*." She kept her voice quiet but persistent. "I'm a lawyer—"

"How well I know, counselor," he interrupted.

"All my cases have to do with employment or housing or equal rights—usually for senior citizens. My kind of practice has bery little to do with banking or corporations in the way Andy thought. Cynthia— and I know all about what she said to Andy—relayed information about a case of mine that involves a banking group. One of the banks in the group is in Kentucky, but she had my role in the matter mixed up," she went on, hearing the note of urgency in her voice. Quickly Kate recapped the suit for him. "So, you see, it isn't a case where my client is a bank—it's a case *against* a banking group." She wanted to touch him but held back. "I don't know what your financial difficulties are but I want to help—if I can. I certainly don't want to hurt you," she said quietly.

Hal was looking down at the floor, his arms still folded. Lydia pushed her nose against his shoulder.

"I've never been anything other than what I said I was, Hal. I took the boat trip for my vacation and it was pure chance that we met. I still feel lucky to have met you." The palomino whinnied from the next stall and stamped her hoof against the floor. "What I feel awful about, in all of this, is that I was afraid to take your feelings and mine seriously—and I didn't even know how much I was doing that. Every time I was with you, I felt the wonder of being with you. You were so candid about the way you felt, but I didn't know exactly how I felt. I dreaded and expected our separation. Pretty soon, I guess the dread outran the expectation." Her need to touch him was so strong now that she had to tighten all the muscles in her arms and then relax them. "My feelings for you are much, much more than I ever allowed myself to show you, than I ever told you about, than I ever imagined—until you were gone. You asked me once how I felt. It was awfully hard to tell you because I really didn't know for sure. So I stumbled through something that sounded inadequate compared to the earthquake going on inside me."

Lydia's soft lips plucked at Hal's breast pocket. She would not let go. He stroked her, then removed two sugar cubes from the pocket and gave them to her.

"Sort of a ritual after the day's over," he explained.

"She's wonderful," Kate said sincerely. "I . . . I've got a lot more to say, Hal. I want to tell you about how I got through law school and why my practice is very important to me. I never really told you, and it's important for you to know. I want you to know how I feel about everything."

"I'd like to believe all that," he finally said. Kate leaned against the outer doorway of the stall, feeling drained.

"I think you know me better than you're admitting right now. You know I couldn't do anything as underhanded as what Cynthia may have implied or as you imagined. It's just not in me."

He moved his feet and pushed Lydia's glossy rump aside so he could stand away from the wall. "Yes, I do know that. At least, that's what I've been telling myself." Lydia turned and gave him a nudge that pushed him toward Kate. Hal smiled crookedly. "You've come a long way to deliver a message."

"I'm not just a messenger, Hal. I had to see you. I wanted to meet this wonderful horse and see the race, too. But it's you I came for."

"You're staying for the race?" he asked, surprised.

"I'd like to. Even if I have to stand on the roof of my rental car in the parking lot by the far turn."

He laughed. "Mighty hard to get good tickets—but Ann will have a few in her hip pocket." His voice, though more relaxed now, still was not the warm, merry expression of him that it had been on the boat, and his eyes were still remote.

Kate glanced around. The horses were settled in for the late afternoon and night.

"Things quiet down here pretty early, don't they?" she noticed.

"Things *start* here very early," he said.

"Will you have dinner with me?"

He hesitated. "Thanks, but I can't. Horses are big but they're delicate, too, and I've got a lot riding on this one." Lydia's intelligent face stared out at them as though fully aware she was under discussion. "Where are you staying?"

"Don't know yet. I came straight from the airport."

"There's a good motel about ten miles down the road. It'll do. You have a car?"

She nodded. She was being dismissed and it hurt. But later, as she got into her car, she realized that he probably needed time. She pulled out of the little parking compound and headed east as Hal had suggested.

But as she checked into the motel, walked to her room, and began to unpack, a vague discomfort clung to her like the dust from the stables. She pushed it away, put her toilet articles in the dressing room, and hung up her clothes. The feeling descended on her again as she called the room clerk to ask for suggestions about where to eat dinner. She didn't really want to eat, but she couldn't stay in the room alone with her thoughts. She sat on the edge of the bed, trying to figure out the source of her feeling.

She'd accomplished what she'd set out to do, and Hal had listened. She'd seen him in his real-life stance and had been as in love with him here as she had been in the middle of the romance of the boat. In fact, she'd had no feelings of mourning the lost riverboat gambler at all; she preferred this struggling, jeans-clad, independent racehorse owner to the debonair gambler. Why did she now feel uneasy and adrift? Because he couldn't—or wouldn't—have dinner? No. But what if he had a lover or fiancée here? Even as that thought crossed her mind, she dismissed it, knowing it wasn't true. Hal was single in the fullest sense of the word. Maybe her expectations for him were unrealistic. Did she want him to welcome her with open arms, kisses, dinner, and bed? That would have been nice but, under the circumstances, impossible. She gave up trying to analyze her predicament.

The restaurant was a white-gabled roadhouse with a tree-shaded parking lot. It looked too elaborate to someone with no appetite, and she was about to pass it by when she saw a large station wagon bearing the Sheffield Stables sign, parked under an oak tree near the front of the lot. Kate pulled in beside it.

What if she found Hal inside? The thought chilled her. If he was there, it might mean that what he'd said to her in the stable had only been a way to put off telling her he didn't want to see her again. She gripped the steering wheel. Would it be better to just drive away? No, she couldn't do that.

It was a warm and comfortable country restaurant with dark wood booths, peg floors, and dim lights.

Curling along one side of the outer room was an oak bar. Ann Sheffield was perched on a stool, wearing a black suit and pearl earrings. A glass next to her signaled an absent companion.

"Hello," Kate said, walking to the bar.

Ann looked around. "Why, hi there. Did you get settled in your motel?"

"Yes, thanks."

"Having dinner?" Ann asked.

"Well, I was thinking about it, but I'm not very hungry. Hal's staying close to Lydia tonight, I understand. Is she ill?"

"Hope not. Probably not." Ann had a clipped but not unpleasant way of speaking. "I think she'll be fine. I told Hal he ought to get out and give Lydia a breather. That horse has run only two races this year. She's probably rarin' to go."

Kate glanced again at the half-full cocktail next to Ann.

"But Hal wouldn't hear of it. That's Hal—a one-track person sometimes. Fears the worst. Got a great horse, though. You heard it here." Ann smiled.

"You mean he's really going to sleep in that stall?"

"Probably. I said I'd bring him back a sandwich."

"I'll do that," Kate offered.

"Want to?" Ann raised her dark eyebrows.

"Sure. I really don't feel like a full dinner, and it'll give me something to do."

"Well, sit down and have a drink."

The only vacant seat was the one next to Ann. Kate glanced at it dubiously. Ann pushed the drink away slightly.

"That's the drink of a guy whose car won't start. You can sit here while he's phoning."

While the sandwiches were being made, Kate learned about Ann's early interest in horses, about her uncle, with whom she did not get along, and how Hal had come to the stables to work for him to pay for Lydia's early schooling. Ann was sharp and quick, and Kate found herself reflecting that the man who trusted a woman trainer would be likely to understand Kate's career needs, too.

As Kate paid for the sandwiches and wine she'd ordered Ann leaned toward her. "Take the back road off the main highway, Kate. That'll put you closer to the stables." Ann's low voice whispered instructions like a coconspirator. "It's going to be dark— watch your step."

Outside the Sheffield Stables, the buildings were lit at various points, but inside the shed, it was dark. Bundling her packages into the crook of her arm, Kate quietly shut the door behind her. A shaded bulb at either end of the stable threw a circle of yellow light over the wood and dust. A horse whinnied gently.

She reached the darkest portion of the stable, equidistant between the two lamps. The horses stirred around her in their stalls, curious, eyes gleaming in the dark shadows as she passed.

Suddenly a figure stepped from one of the far stalls into the center. The light behind him outlined his stance: legs spread wide, hands on hips, head tilted slightly to the left. It was Hal.

Kate stopped. She did not want him to feel her intense excitement as she knew he would the moment she stepped back into the light. Hal, too, remained motionless. She began to feel strands of thick silence spool out between them. A horse snorted and broke the gathering spell. He dropped his arms and started toward her. She clutched the bag to her, wishing she could read his face, but the light was behind him, and even as he stopped before her—so close she could feel his warm breath—his face was still in shadow. He reached out and took the package from her, putting it on the ground. For an instant, the light flashed on his profile as he straightened, then the shadows enveloped him. She felt his fingertips on her arm.

"So. You return," he said.

"Yes," she breathed, acutely aware that the lamp now lighted her face plainly.

One hand lifted her chin as his shadowed face seemed to examine hers minutely. His fingers curled around her cheek. Then, very slowly and gently, he bent to taste her lips before kissing them. She thought she felt a shudder of relief pass through his body, but perhaps it was through her own. His arms folded around her. He kissed her eyes, her earlobes, and her throat.

"Oh, God, how I've missed you," he said, his lips against her cheek. "I was sure you wouldn't come back, that you'd go on to San Francisco. I just couldn't say what I wanted to today when I saw you standing there near the paddock. And I don't even care what's happened, though I wouldn't have blamed you if you'd left."

"Oh, Hal, how could I have not come?" she moaned, putting her head in the hollow of his shoulder and feeling her thighs against his. "I feel so close to you."

Gently he released her and led her by the hand down the darkened row of stalls into one that was empty. "Watch your step here," he said, guiding her. It was quite dark except for the dim yellow glow of the lamp farther down the corridor. She could make out only a hammock and a mound of straw beside it.

The straw felt surprisingly springy as he drew her down upon it, brushing a strand of her hair back from her forehead. As she reached out for him they seized each other with tremendous force, rocking and holding and kissing wildly. When she was finally able to relax against his arm curled around her waist, she opened herself to a river of ripe sensations that she had feared she would never feel with him again. Somehow, her sweater and blouse were open, releasing her breasts to the dim glow and cool night air. His lips found them. His other hand swept around the small of her back, raising her to him. She quivered. Her body felt on fire as he pressed her into the giving, scented hay. Then he raised his head from her breast and pulled her toward the hollow of his shoulder, one hand behind her head, holding her.

"Never go away," he breathed, "never go away."

She tugged at his chin with her fingertips and drew his lips to hers, nibbling at them. It was life-giving to be so close to him again. His tongue reached inside her mouth and her chest tightened. She could not stop her hand from trembling as she unbuttoned his shirt and slipped her hand inside, across the downy hair. Her mouth followed her hand. He reared back and struggled out of his shirt.

In a moment he slid out of his clothes and lay naked against her, reaching for her. As he sought her lips again she wondered at how different this was compared to the other times they had made love. They clung ecstatically as they expressed their relief and desire. The darkness hid his long, searching glances, as well as his gestures, so that she never knew where he would touch her next. The erotic darkness enveloped them. She was drowning in his kisses and her own need, and each shudder of pleasure that he drew from her body widened the pool of her overwhelming sensations. He was in her and all around her, engulfing her with his fervent hunger, kissing her shoulders and breasts and belly. She arched under the assault as the heat rippled through her body. This time there would be no words.

Now he was over her; her fingers gripped his damp hair, drawing his mouth to hers again, colliding and releasing in longer and longer spasms as they strained and fought to become one till the final ecstatic collision, which merged them completely.

Later, she lay in the hammock, his jacket tossed over her. He leaned against the wall of the stall and poured them each a glass of the red wine she had brought.

"Yes," he whispered, reading her thoughts, "I am still vulnerable to you."

"I wasn't thinking that exactly. But I'm glad to hear you care about me."

"To be vulnerable is not always to care," he said.

"I know. But, nevertheless, you *do* care."

"Yes," he said, "I do." She took the glass. The hammock felt precarious, stretched across the corner, but it had a gentle, lazy swing to it, and she felt safe in his arms. He stroked her head. "How do you feel?" he asked softly.

"Wonderful—especially considering what I expected to find tonight."

"What was that?"

"Cold shoulder. Short comments. Silence."

"I thought a lot about what you said this afternoon." He sighed. "I behaved like a damn fool. I'm really surprised you came back tonight."

"Do you remember what you said when you told me you loved me in the park?"

"What?"

"You said, 'What are you going to do about it?'"

"Oh, yes," He waited for her to speak, and when she didn't, he said, "Guess that question still holds, doesn't it?"

"Yup," she said, mimicking him gently.

"Well, counselor, I don't know what you're going to do, but I can tell you what I want."

"Good enough."

"I want you to stay here. I don't ever want you to go away because . . . His voice grew hoarse and his hand, which had been smoothing her hair, stopped moving. "Because I don't think I can live without you, Kate."

The stable seemed to close in around her as she blindly reached out for him. "Oh, Hal, Hal." She felt so moved she was close to tears. "I want it to be good for both of us. But I'd be lying to you if I said I could just phone San Francisco and tell them I'm never coming back, and stay here and never work again."

"I know that. I understand, Kate." He moved away from her, trailing an arm from her waist and moving one hand back to smooth her hair from her temple. "Let's do this: you stay till the derby."

"Try and stop me. What else?"

"We'll find a compromise."

"Live in Colorado?" she asked archly.

"No, silly. A real compromise, not just a geographic one."

Lydia stirred in the next stall. "How is she?" Kate asked.

"Seems good. We'll know tomorrow. If she's better, we'll go to the track."

"You mean Churchill Downs? But the race isn't till Saturday."

"The racers get there early." He rubbed her shoulders. "Do I have an answer, counselor?"

"To . . ."

"Working it out."

"Of course, I want to work it out. That's why I'm here, idiot."

Suddenly she yawned, feeling a lazy contentment slip over her. He took the glass from her hand, then kissed her. His deep voice seemed to come from very far away.

"I'm glad you're here," he whispered. Just before she fell asleep, she knew that the Hal she'd feared lost had returned to her. Or was it she who had returned to him?

Chapter Ten

❧

Hal woke her before dawn.

"Come on. We're going for breakfast before everyone finds you literally sacked out in the hay."

They went to an all-night truckers' stop and ate piles of eggs and grits washed down with steaming coffee. She thought at moments that Hal was trying to conceal his happiness, for when he imagined she wasn't looking at him, the luminous glances he shot at her gave him away. She felt a delicious mixture of joy and apprehension.

In the car, as she drove back to the stables, he reached across to touch her. "I'm so glad you're here. We'll just take things one step at a time. Okay?"

She nodded. He had instantly put her at ease again.

The stable was alive with trainers, walkers, jockeys, and grooms—all busy with a dozen different tasks centered around their expensive aristocratic charges.

"I think I'll go back to the motel and change," Kate said as they walked down to the training track.

"No, no, stay and see how she rates," he urged her. "You look beautiful. Rumpled—but beautiful." He smiled winningly. "She's a worker," he went on in a different tone, "but if she's got some of the prankster back in her this morning, she's on the mend."

The grooms were leading a few horses, Lydia among them, out onto the track. Lydia's jockey saluted Hal, who took out his stopwatch. Ann came up beside them.

"Good morning, you two," she said, casting a quick glance at each of them. "How's she look?"

"Good," Hal said.

"She looks a little small compared to those other horses," Kate replied.

Ann replied, "A horse is too large or too small only if it can't run fast enough or far enough."

Other people around the paddock were coming down to the track.

"Barney, Mel," Hal greeted two of them, "how goes it? Want you to meet Kate Sewell." The men nodded at her. Barney's last name was Sheffield, so Kate assumed that he was Ann's uncle. He was a burly man with long sideburns and a mustache; his jeans were pulled tight under his pot belly and he had an air of authority that was not completely friendly.

Kate turned her attention to the track. Lydia *did* look the part of an eager racer and she seemed positively frisky. At the signal, they were off, and for Kate, it was an unexpected thrill to see her race, easily leading the small field, head high. As she came around the turn both Hal and Ann raised their stopwatches. Lydia dashed past them. The watches clicked off in unison, and Hal looked at Ann.

"Did she rate well?" Kate asked.

"She sure did."

Lydia, though slowing, was still pounding lightly and happily down the track.

"What happens now?"

"She'll be cooled out," said Hal, washed, dried, blanketed, and led back for breakfast." He looked at Kate. "You'd better start getting a feel for all this." He took her arm and winked at Ann. "I'm trying to make a horsewoman out of this lawyer."

Ann was about to say something, then stopped, looking at Kate shrewdly. Hal was oblivious.

"Come on," he said happily, "I want to look at her."

A half hour later, Kate held the reins as she and Hal walked Lydia to cool her down. Hal was exuberant.

"Doesn't she look the part?" he asked.

"Hal, she's wonderful."

Hal stopped and took the reins from her. "Do you really like her, Kate—I mean really?"

"Yes, I do," Kate said. "How could anyone not like such a beautiful animal?" After a moment she said, "It's amazing—you fit into this life as well as you did into life on the boat."

"I'm glad to hear it," he exclaimed, leading Lydia and putting his arm about Kate's waist. "No man is happier than I am at this moment," he said. Lydia whinnied softly as though in agreement. Kate stroked her fine, glossy neck, knowing that Lydia had it in her power to change Hal's life.

By the time Lydia had her rubdown, she looked and behaved as though she could run the derby in a minute flat. The vet pronounced her ready to race and Hal threw his hat into the air with a whoop.

It was noon. Kate suggested they lunch, but Hal

had to work with Ann over final arrangements for the race. He placed his palm against her cheek. "I know you want to talk and that all this is very boring for you—"

"Honestly, Hal, it's *not* boring. How could you think it was?"

"Well, I don't know," he said, suddenly serious. "You just looked bored. I'm glad you're not. I'm very proud of everything here"—he swept one arm out—"and I want you to be interested in it."

"I was distracted. That's all."

"Okay," he said, taken aback.

Kate searched his face. How could their lives possibly fit together? If she could see any way other than total capitulation to his life-style, she would dive after it and make it work. But already she knew that just being Hal's sidekick wouldn't be enough.

Rather than try to discuss the issue now, when he was so busy, she told him she would meet him later, and she headed back to the motel to change into her jeans and a jacket.

The main room of the ranch house served as an office and waiting room for the business of the stables. It was about two o'clock when Kate walked into it and came face to face with two sheriff's deputies.

"I can't believe it," Ann was saying, fairly spitting the words out. "Lou Foss couldn't possibly do this."

Kate stopped just inside the door. One of the deputies stood rigidly while the other shuffled his feet uncomfortably, embarrassed.

"Aw, Ann—Jake and me didn't have anything to do with this—"

"I know, Bobby," Hal said. His voice, to Kate, was

outwardly calm, but she could hear the tremor of anger beneath the words.

Kate stepped forward and her eyes met Hal's.

"Kate," he said, "we're doing a little business here. I'll join you in a moment."

"I'm sorry, Hal," Bobby said. "I know how you feel about the filly and she sure is a sweet-looking horse."

"You are required to appear—"

"Skip it, Jake," said Bobby. "He knows, for God's sake."

"What's going on?" Kate asked.

The deputies turned to her, but Hal turned away. Ann stared at Kate, then looked back at Hal, who had walked toward a window.

"Well?" asked Kate.

Hal spun toward her. She had never seen him so angry. "The bank is *seizing the collateral* for nonpayment of my loan."

"Why didn't you tell me this was in the offing before now?" Ann broke in, striding up to Hal.

"And what could you have done? Mortgaged your stable? Sold a horse?" he asked her cynically.

"You know I couldn't—it's not my decision. But perhaps I could have talked with Lou Foss—"

"Who's he?" asked Kate.

"The president of the bank," Hal said impatiently. "It's not a great big bank like they have in California. Kate, just a little one, run by its president."

"And the collateral is Lydia?"

"Yes, after I'd mortgaged my land."

"What's the amount due?"

"A total of nearly a hundred thousand dollars, and I have stiff payments on it each month."

"In racing and owner terms," Ann broke in again,

"that's not much. His expenses would have been a lot greater if Lydia hadn't won races, which helped pay the costs."

The deputies glanced at Kate curiously.

"Does she have an interest in this matter?" Jake asked.

"Yes," Kate said. "I am Mr. Lewis's attorney."

Her declaration seemed to stun the small group. Jake huffed as though he'd known it all along. Bobby and Ann looked pleasantly surprised. Kate saw Hal's face open in a funny way as a constellation of expressions unfolded: he was surprised, but she also saw pride and hope.

"That's a trump, isn't it?" Kate said to the deputies. "Are you two here to take the horse?"

"Yes, ma'am, that's right," said Jake.

"Okay, here's what we're going to do," Kate said briskly. "You can take the horse if your papers are in order—"

"*Kate*," Hal exclaimed. "You're just going to hand Lydia over to them?"

"Let me finish, Hal." She turned back to the deputies.

"You can take the horse, but I'll go right down to court and get a temporary restraining order, which will prevent you from taking any action until a judge hears both sides. That's a lot of backing and forthing, and the horse will have to be cared for in the meantime. I have a better idea. You two take me down to the bank to see Mr. Foss." The deputies nodded. "I'd like to have a little chat with him. I am sure we can work out an equitable arrangement." Kate smiled.

*   *   *

Mr. Foss's office was in a new building that housed the bank and other businesses. Though his secretary had told her he would see her as soon as she arrived, he kept her waiting in the outer office for almost half an hour.

Foss was a small, bony man, about sixty-five. Judging by his cold eyes and sharp features, Kate thought he'd be a peppery man of decided opinions. He leaned back in his chair and took Kate in as she strode across the carpeted room. She knew from the look of him that he'd be a hard bargainer.

"Mr. Foss?" Kate extended her hand.

"That's right." He rose, shaking her hand gingerly. "Sit down, Miss Sewell."

Kate looked around the room as Foss pulled out a file from a stack on the right-hand side of the desk. The room was quite modern, much more so than she thought would appeal to a conservative banker in the South.

"So you're Hal Lewis's attorney," he began.

"That's right. We've got—"

"Pretty young for a lawyer, aren't you?"

"Old enough, Mr. Foss. I've come to see you about a horse." She smiled and actually saw the flicker of a smile from him.

"Pretty good horse," he said laconically. "I'll tell you right out front that I'm sorry Hal's got himself in so much deep water over this. I've got no use for the horse. The bank will just auction it. But we can't make any exceptions here—it'd be all over town, if we did. He's not able to pay—that's been demonstrated—and we're in the lending business, as you might know, not in the investment business."

"Sure. I have—"

"And another thing, I must tell you. I don't like lady lawyers."

"Why not think of me as Hal's representative in this matter?"

He considered this. "You're speaking for him? What you say will be binding for him?"

"That's the way it is. I'd like to work out a plan so that you and Hal can both get what you want."

Foss cackled delightedly, then stopped abruptly.

"Impossible," he said.

"Maybe not." Kate wanted to fold her arms across her chest, where Foss's eyes had now settled, but she restrained herself: it would look too defensive. She compromised and folded her hands in her lap. Casually she went on: "You don't want to race the horse, you said, and Hal does. You'll just sell it but you'll be losing out on sweeping up the filly's best and soonest purse."

"Not so," he broke in. "The sale won't take long. It's a straight business transaction, Miss Sewell."

"Yes, but it's got a major wrinkle in it, Mr. Foss."

He looked at her doubtfully and sighed.

"You see, if you take the filly today or tomorrow, she stands a good chance of losing the race."

"Hogwash."

"I don't think so, Mr. Foss." Kate spoke forcefully. "The horse is a thoroughbred—high strung and intelligent. You know how difficult horses can be." His sudden frown indicated that he'd had firsthand experience with difficult horses. "This one's mother died twenty days after she was born."

"Really, Miss Sewell, you'll get no tears from me on that score."

"Don't expect any. But you should know that Hal

raised this filly like a parent raises a child, and from what I know from his trainer—Ann Sheffield—they are much closer than the usual owner and racehorse. Now, you take this horse out of Sheffield's, away from Hal, move it to another stable, and put a whole new set of people around her—and I think you will agree . . ."

"Agree about what?"

"That you stand a good chance of rattling her enough so that she won't win, rather, won't have the same chance to win that she would have had—had you left her with Hal."

Foss was eyeing her narrowly. "A very convenient argument, Miss Sewell."

"I realize that it sounds a little sentimental, but in this particular case, it's really good business to consider some of the elements that contribute to the overall situation."

"So," Foss said after a long silence. "What's your proposition—though I'm going to tell you I think it's all hocus-pocus so far."

"My proposition is this," Kate said brightly, knowing that his critical objections were placed in her path mainly to break her concentration and make her chase down dead ends. She was not going to do that, but she couldn't tell if he would play hard banker or just hard ball. He seemed impenetrable.

"If you wait until after the derby, and if the horse wins, places, or shows, I will guarantee—as Hal Lewis's legal representative—repayment of the full amount by thirty days after the race."

"Lot of ifs in that proposition."

"Some, but not an unacceptable number, I would

think, considering the great benefits that would be yours—and Hal's—in so short a time."

"What if she doesn't even show?"

"The second part of my proposition. That we renegotiate a schedule of payments to you right now—"

"No, no, no, that's no good. I can take the horse right now. Why should I agree to a new schedule when he can't pay now? It's absurd."

"That's debatable. Let's stick to what's probable."

"It's probable that he won't pay, since he can't pay now." Foss slapped the file on his desk.

"It's probable the filly will stand a better chance in the derby if she stays with Hal. It's probable she will win other races even if she doesn't win the derby. It's probable she will always win more frequently with Hal than without him. Always. It's been proved she wins races, that she's an unusually good racehorse, or she wouldn't even be in the derby." Kate wished she had a lot more information about how horses were accepted in the derby, and more about Lydia's own racing record. Kate was pulling on every piece of information Hal had told her about racing to keep up her end of this negotiation. "Hal told me just before I left that he would sell the land he owns if she doesn't at least show. It won't get you the whole hundred thousand, but it ought to net about thirty-five thousand, and at that point—or now—I'll set up a schedule with you, based on the filly's projected earnings, plus the net sale of the property, so that you are repaid promptly. But frankly I don't think any of this will be necessary because I think she's going to win." Kate wished she were really as confident as she pretended to be.

"Very sure of that, aren't you?" Foss tapped his letter opener lightly against the edge of the desk.

Kate gave him a moment, then said in an entirely different tone, "Very pleasant office you have here. Is everything new?"

"Yes," he said tightly.

Kate surveyed Foss carefully. "Did you recently move?"

"Yes. We had a fine office in the original building down the street—high ceilings, marble. Building with history and standards ... Well, is that your proposition?"

"I can picture you in that kind of office," she said sincerely. "This one seems a little—"

"Racy," he supplied. "Don't like these modern lamps much. Decorators, you know."

"I was going to say chilly." She glanced at the streamlined sofa.

"Most people think bankers *are* cold, Miss Sewell."

"Yes, but that's because they confuse good business sense with coldness," she said.

Foss sent her a wan smile. "Guess they teach you people something out there in California ... You like antiques?"

"Yes, very much."

Pointing to a burled wood and crystal inkstand on his desk, he told her where it had been made, by whom, how old it was, and where he'd bought it. As he spoke she realized that he was turning her proposal over in his mind and, at the same time, evaluating her. Her instincts told her to say nothing at this moment but to let him take his time. The inkwell afforded them at least five minutes of conversation.

But by the time it was tapped out, Foss lost some of his critical manner.

"So, what you want is to hold it all off a bit, in essence," he said.

"In a way, but with a firm agreement that's bound to get you the money you are due and will keep the filly with Hal, where she's going to earn everyone the most money. I also want to seal it with a schedule so that you are guaranteed to be paid, not left hanging. And I have Hal's agreement to this."

"He made me furious," Foss suddenly snapped. "We already *had* such an agreement—it's called a *loan*. He didn't tell me he was having problems, he didn't answer the loan officer's letters—he just ignored the whole thing."

Very calmly, Kate said, "I know Mr. Foss, and I apologize for Mr. Lewis."

"You let him make his own apologies, miss."

"Hal is not a good businessman, but he does know horses. In the future his knowledge and your experience might be profitable for both of you."

"I'm not interested in making profits off some poor guy with a horse. I'm interested in solid, reputable business transactions with solid, reputable business people."

Kate was confident now that she knew the root of the problem: Mr. Foss was hurt and insulted.

"Mr. Foss, you know that if Lady Lydia wins the derby, Hal will be an owner with a reputation, not just hopes. I think, thanks to your move this afternoon, that he's learned a valuable lesson about business and that he's going to make sure he has good business advice in the future, just as he has the advice of a good trainer. He's at a turning point right now and it's in your hands."

Kate was pulling out of the bank's parking lot when it struck her. In transactions like the one with Foss, she was comfortable and on solid emotional ground. She had spent years training for confrontations and negotiations, listening for nuances and looking at body language. But in all that time she had completely neglected the emotional side of her nature. Not once had she been swept off her feet. Not once had she been so completely captivated by a man as she was now. And that, she said to herself as she pulled out onto the avenue, was why she felt so at sea with Hal and so conflicted. She had a lot to learn.

When Kate returned to the stables, it was past five o'clock. The soft dusk of spring was settling over the hills and pastures. Kate felt exhilarated as she headed in the main building, calling, "Ann. Hal."

She heard voices from a back room. The door opened. Hal stood in the light, Ann behind him. Kate savored the moment and looked from one to the other, then turned and walked into the large outer room. They followed.

"Don't keep us hanging in suspense—how was your meeting?" Hal asked lightly. Kate knew that he felt anything but casual. She composed her face and turned. "Oh," he said, seeing her expression, "didn't work, huh? Well, Foss is a tough dealer. I'm sure you did your best."

"That's okay," Ann chimed in.

Kate let out the laugh of triumph. She could feel her whole face changing.

"Yes, he *is* a good dealer, but we have our deal."

Amazement lit Hal's face and he yelled and took her in his arms. Ann clapped and cheered. "I can't believe it," Hal kept saying. "How'd you *do* it?" He stopped squeezing Kate and put her at arm's length, his hands gripping her shoulders tightly. "You are terrific, absolutely terrific. I suppose you want to have a business talk."

"Yes," she said, seeing him look at her with new respect.

Ann said, "Shall I break out the champagne?"

"Don't you want to hear the deal? Maybe you won't like it."

"Does Lydia stay?" asked Hal.

"She does."

"Then I like it."

"How about the rest of it?" asked Ann, a little more cautiously.

"If she doesn't win, place, or show—which would give you the purse to pay off the bank—you have to sell the land you own, Hal, or sign it over to the bank, plus deduct regular amounts from her future winnings until the loan is paid off."

"How'd you get him to take any risk with us on her future winnings? Oh, never mind. I have no head for business at all, and I know I haven't played my cards well." He flashed Kate that quick, intimate look that pierced her heart. "Now there's even more riding on her back, isn't there?"

"Afraid so. But, you know, the real problem was that Foss was insulted that you hadn't come to him when you got into trouble on the payments."

"A banker's insulted?" he asked, incredulous.

"Sure. They're just like other people—they have feelings."

"Well, maybe a few do."

"Anyway, that's the deal. Are you going to accept it?"

Hal stared at her. "Of course I am. And she is going to *win*."

Ann snorted. "Better keep this one around, Hal," she said, indicating Kate, "before you lose your shirt as well as your horse."

"No, no, just a good deed done for my friend, here." Kate laughed, then saw the deflated look on Hal's face. "Oh, Hal, I didn't mean to sound flippant." She went up to him.

"I'll get that champagne," Ann said tactfully, then darted out of the room.

"Is that the *only* reason you did this helpful deed?" he asked. His soft, brown eyes seemed to bore into her and his outstretched arms held her firmly. "Tell me," he said gently. His hands slipped from her shoulders to her elbows. She felt the spell of him and her love for him envelop her.

"No," she whispered. "Of course not. I did it because I love you, Hal, and because I thought that through it, I might find a way to stay with you. At least for us to have a life together."

He shivered. "And have you?"

"I'm not sure yet."

"Are you sure of anything?"

"I'm sure I love you. And I'm sure I don't know much about love," she added, thinking of the drive back from Foss's bank. She sighed, and it felt cleansing. Hal gathered her into his arms and held her close.

"You love me?" he breathed.

"I love you."

"Then we can learn together if—"

"Champagne," Anne cried from the doorway, but Hal, unmoving, kept his eyes on Kate.

"I will not, nor could I, force you to do anything you don't want to do. But I hope we can find a way. I don't want to live without you."

He leaned forward and kissed her with much tenderness then pulled away reluctantly. "Champagne?" he whispered. "*Champagne*," he shouted jubilantly, "to toast my attorney."

Chapter Eleven

❧

"I can't sleep," Hal said. It was the night before the race. "I'm too keyed up." He paced to the window of their hotel room and stared out, his hands thrust into the pockets of his robe.

Kate went up to him, put her arms around his waist, and leaned her head against his back. His body felt taut, the muscles rigid with tension.

"Come to bed. Even if you don't sleep, it will do you good to lie down and rest," she said. Kate started to untie his robe, but he put his hands over hers.

"Don't."

"You must get some rest, Hal."

"I couldn't sleep if someone knocked me on the head with a hammer."

"I love you, Hal," she said, but her thoughts did not reflect the certainty of her words. If she did not move to Kentucky, what did that say about her love for him? she wondered. Where is it written that I have to choose between my work and my love? If I choose one, do I stop loving the other? In the days since she'd been with him in Kentucky, they had talked whenever they could, and she had shared more about herself than she ever had. But the week packed with frenetic preparations for the race.

"Where are you, Kate?" he asked softly. She looked up and smiled wanly.

"Here."

"How can I convince such a stubborn, dedicated woman that she belongs here with me, not back in California?" She shrugged prettily. "I have tried everything a poor old boy like me knows to move you inland. But I'm at my wit's end."

"It's not that I don't want to live here with you, Hal. It's taken me years to begin to build up my professional contracts in San Francisco. Why don't you just move to California?" She played with the lapels of his bathrobe.

He smiled and sighed. They had driven this road before. "God, I can't believe how much is riding on her tomorrow," he said, remotely but passionately. "My little plot of land, my future, her future, your future . . ."

"Whether she wins or loses, it won't change how I feel about you. You do know that, don't you?"

"Yes, my love, I do now. But if she doesn't finish in the money—"

"You'll sell the land. You'll race her elsewhere— say, California—and she'll win as she has before. And you'll pay off the bank. The world won't end."

"If she doesn't finish in the money, a lot of *my* world will end."

"But she will win other races."

"You don't understand," he cried out. "She *has* to win this one. That's what I've mortgaged and borrowed and worked for. This is only the first step."

Hal seemed desperate, far beyond what she would have expected even in these unusual circumstances.

"What do you mean?"

Very softly, he answered, "I've entered her in the Preakness . . . And in the Belmont."

Kate's face went slack with surprise. "God, I'm so new to all this, I never thought to ask. How much is your total debt?"

"About a hundred and fifty thousand," he finally admitted, moving away from her. "Every dime she's earned has been put back into nomination fees, post fees, entry fees, vet bills, insurance . . . and she was off for about four months last fall."

"How much do you owe Ann?" Kate asked, beginning to piece the appalling picture together.

"A lot. I couldn't have done it unless she'd carried me. But if I don't pay the stables off soon, if I don't at least get a show tomorrow, Ann's uncle will toss me out. He's been waiting to do it, and it's part of the strain between him and Ann."

Kate ran a hand through her hair. "I'm glad I didn't know you were going for the Triple when I talked to Foss," she muttered, staring at the man she loved with a kind of awe. Hal touched her cheek with the back of his palm.

"When I gamble, Kate, I go for it all," he said. "Are you shocked? Does it make me less to you?"

"I'm surprised, I guess. More than that—astonished."

"But does it make me less in your eyes—this reckless nickle-and-diming my way to the top?" He gripped her shoulders urgently.

For the first time she saw wrinkles at the outer corners of his eyes. "I believe you'll get to the top,

Hal. There certainly is no turning back." She felt her chest tighten; it was hard to take it all in. Everything seemed to have shifted.

Hal folded her into his arms. "I will understand if this is more than you bargained for, Kate. God knows, it's more than I bargained for."

But for some crazy reason Kate was beginning to feel exhilarated. She couldn't have explained it but she suddenly respected him more. Yes, he'd taken a lunatic risk, but she admired his imagination and his courage.

"From big risks come big prizes," Kate said quietly. "But you need a backer, Hal—*several* backers. You can't just hang out there all by yourself."

"You're my biggest gamble," he stated unequivocably, "and I hope you're my biggest backer. When I met you again on the boat, I knew you were something special. I tried to back off," he continued. "Not because of my job there, but because I knew I was falling in love with you that first night. How could I ask you to become a part of this kind of madness? There I was, a man with a horse and a hundred and fifty thousand dollars in debt. My chances to win just one race of the Triple Crown were—minute. Could I ask you to be a party to such a great risk? I didn't think I could. But I couldn't stop reaching out for you. I couldn't push away my feelings for you, and I couldn't say, Oh, well, I'll see her in California sometime when all this is settled . . . Though, believe me, I tried." He gripped her arms. "You made me feel alive and that all the risks were worthwhile." His voice shook and she could feel the tremor in his arms.

A silence fell between them as each sank into his own thoughts.

"I was talking to Ann today," Hal finally said. "Since the old man's back now, she's one down as usual. She wants her own place. She wants out from under."

"Where? Here in Kentucky?"

"Yes. She's beginning to ask owners to go in with her."

"And she's asked you," Kate said.

"Yes. It would be a fine outfit, small at first, but size isn't everything. Kate, racing's a business as well as a sport and a skill. But I don't have any talent for business."

"Hal, it's just not my role in life to . . . to run a business, if that's what you are leading up to."

"But don't you think that we're better as a team?" A jagged smile started to form on either side of his mouth.

"I *know* we're better as a team." She laughed.

"You know that, huh?" He rached out to brush his fist against her jaw. His eyes held her. She loved nothing more than to sit quietly with him and lose herself in his eyes. He took her hand again and gently spread her fingers apart, one by one. She started to speak, but he stopped her.

"Don't say anything. It's your great weakness."

It was getting easier to slip inside that delicious world of sensation that he or her emotions, or both, brought on. She welcomed its warmth as a balm.

"No evasions," he warned gently.

"I'm not," she said, thinking about Ann, the prospect of a new stable, Hal's outrageous gamble on the Triple, and where she, Kate, might fit into it all.

"You're really hanging out there to dry, aren't you?" she finally asked, but it was really no question. Hal didn't answer. "I think I have an idea for a compromise." Hal looked up sharply. "You need to partner this horse."

Hal looked deflated. "Of course I need to partner the horse, Kate. But I'm not going to do that until after the race."

"An Ann needs a partner for her stables if she's decided to break with her uncle."

"Yes," he said, more attentively now.

"What if I could find you both an investor partner?"

"Where do you fit in?"

"With you, Hal. I'm not leaving you in such a fix—win, lose, or draw."

His arm looped out for her waist. "You'll stay here?"

"I don't know if it will be here or there. But let me work a few things out—is that okay with you for now? And we'll talk after the race. The only thing I really wanted to tell you right now is that I don't want to live without you, either. If you'll compromise a little, we'll get this act together."

Hal pulled her toward him and kissed her warmly, his arms wrapped tightly around her. "I feel as if I'm dreaming. Are you really saying that you'll stay? Do you mean it?"

"Yes. I want you to know that before the race tomorrow."

"I don't get it but I don't care."

"How would it look if you won and I suddenly decided to stay?" she asked. "Or how would it look if you lost and I suddenly decided to leave?"

"Why, you little gold digger," he said teasingly.

"See? That's why I wanted you to know now." She could feel her body trembling as he pressed her to him and sought her lips. Finally she coaxed him into bed and held him in her arms, trying to think what was best to do.

About two in the morning, he rose. "I've got to go over to the track, Kate," he murmured.

"Now? Security's tight over there, Hal, and Lydia's fine. Come back to bed . . . please."

At last she persuaded him, but at dawn she could restrain him no longer. After he'd left, she dialed room service and ordered coffee. Then she leaned back against the pillows and started formulating the plan that was beginning to take shape in her mind.

Kate stood with Ann in the saddling area looking down at the first horse to come in from the barn—a huge black one who rolled his eyes imperiously.

"That's Lombardy," Ann shouted as a hubbub arose on all sides of the room. Spectators lined the rail of the upper tier, and the lower level swarmed with grooms, trainers, and officials. As each horse arrived from the sheds a groom led it to an open stall so that everyone, above and on ground level, could see the saddling.

"There she is," cried Kate. Lydia had pranced into the room, head high. She was clearly excited and her coat shone like satin. A groom led her around to her stall, where one of Sheffield's assistant trainers began to saddle her. "Is she weighted?" Kate asked Ann.

"Sure. There are small lead bars in the pockets of her saddlebags."

The saddle looked like a small dish. Kate knew it

weighed only about three pounds, since everything was designed for lightness. The assistant secured the saddle with an elasticized girth, then he hiked up the second girth, which went on top of the saddle to make sure it wouldn't slip during the race.

"What's next?" Kate asked.

"Hal will give Tim some last-minute instructions, Lydia will be checked over, and then she's led out onto the track. There's Tim," Ann said, pointing below. He had ridden her for her last win, and Hal was thankful that he could ride Lydia in this all-important race.

"It's a real honor to ride in the derby, isn't it?"

"Sure is, and more dough for the jockey if she finishes in the money. He's a very good jock, but a filly in the derby is a long shot no matter how good she appears to be. Lombardy's the favorite—big, strong colt."

"I read that in his last race he took the lead in the upper stretch and pulled away by two lengths, holding it all the way home," Kate said somewhat haltingly.

Ann looked at her. "My, there's hope for you yet, Kate. Did you memorize that?" She laughed.

"Pretty nearly. I wanted to start getting the lingo down . . . What's it really take to win, Ann?"

"The will to dominate the field."

Kate thought about this a moment, then said, "Ann, Hal tells me you're thinking of starting your own stables. Would you be adverse to doing that in Southern California if I could find you an investor out there?"

Ann looked at her squarely. "I'd be a fool to say no."

"But could you—would you like to—operate out there?"

"Out there? You make it sound like the other side of the sun. There are a lot of good tracks there—Santa Anita, Del Mar, Hollywood Park. What's up?"

"I'm trying to find a way for Hal and me to stay together, and I know he wants to go in with you on the stables."

"And you can't live here, can you?"

"No, Ann, I really can't."

"I'd love Southern California but I never thought of it 'cause I don't know anyone out there. But this is a little premature—isn't it? If Lydia doesn't at least show in this race, Hal is done for. And he won't be partnering with anyone." Ann glanced around. "Listen, I have to go now. See you in the box. We'll talk later."

And she was gone. Kate scanned the room below and finally located Hal standing near one corner, arms folded, looking grim. His eyes never left Lydia and Kate knew he was sizing her up as she was led out of her stall to the paddock circle to be mounted. Lydia's hind legs pushed down against the floor, rippling the muscles in her haunches.

Kate reached the box to find Barney Sheffield and two other owners connected with his stables already seated. A few minutes later, Ann arrived with Hal, who was so keyed up he could barely speak.

"How's our horse?" asked Kate.

"Our horse?" Hal replied, as though from the depths of a dream. He sat down next to Kate and took out his binoculars to focus them on the track.

"How's Tim?" Kate asked in an effort to calm Hal down. His hands were shaking.

"He's okay, he knows her. He'll give her her head. She's a strayer." Sheffield snorted rudely from the other side of the box. "I just put it in Tim's hands," Hal continued. "He'll play it right."

"She's in the outside post position," Kate said worriedly. "That's not good, is it?"

"For some horses it would be bad, but not necessarily for Lydia. I feel okay about that."

"Lombardy's five to seven," someone said.

Ann touched Kate's shoulder. "Lydia's a great horse to ride. No trouble in the gates, and you don't have to whip her—she's not a stick horse. I only hope she breaks with a clear path."

"Yes," said Hal, "so do I." He gave Kate a quick, nervous smile, then raised his glasses and said, "Post parade," under his breath.

A cry went up from the packed stands as the first horse and its lead pony came onto the track. It was Lombardy, an easy horse to spot, since he was black and large. Lombardy had drawn the rail position, which, Ann had told Kate, would make him even stronger competition. Since he was not a distance runner, the rail position gave him the shortest race to run around the track. Lombardy walked calmly, nose to the flank of his lead pony. A horse behind him cantered sideways, rolling its eyes back toward the paddock, and the horse behind that one seemed to gape at the crowd at the rail. The jockeys were crouched on their mounts, knees bent, bright colors catching the light of this idyllic sunny day.

"Doesn't she look great?" cried Kate as Lydia jogged out onto the track, tail flicking. Hal only nodded. They were almost to the starting gate. Kate felt so choked up she could hardly breathe. The crowd below seemed to move forward as a body, and the railbirds—the people standing down by the rail at the edge of the track—craned their necks and shoved their arms, holding tickets and rolled programs out toward the horses. Across from the paddock, two red-, yellow-, and blue-striped poles proclaimed the finish line. It was pageantry, Kate thought, no doubt about it. She felt the high, suffocating tension born of the certain knowledge that the next five minutes could bring fame, wealth, disappointment, ruin, death, injury, triumph.

The horse next to Lydia—Marble Archer—was being shoved into its position as Lydia stepped with dignity into her spot in the gate. Kate glanced sideways at Hal; his eyes were glued to his glasses, the knuckles of his hands white. She saw Ann wink at her, then lift her binoculars. At that moment Kate heard the loudspeaker blare, the clang of the gates opening and when she turned around—they were off.

Lombardy seized the lead at the rail, and Marble Archer was second, deliberately keeping wide to prevent Lydia from cutting in toward the rail. The other horses had bunched up behind Lombardy.

"She broke badly," cried Ann desperately.

Lydia seemed not to be in the race at all, but on the edge of it. At the quarter-mile turn, Lombardy was still in the lead, Marble Archer second, another horse third. Lydia, to Kate's eye, just barely seemed to be getting her rhythm in fourth place. As Tim, the jockey, said later, "I took her out to keep her away from the others. I wanted her to calm down."

Kate didn't remember when she jumped to her feet but she was on them now, yelling at the top of her lungs. At the half mile, Marble Archer was coming on very strong, edging the lead away from the favorite, Lombardy, and Lydia was more than ten lengths behind them, still on the outside. But even Kate could now see she was running evenly, hitting her stride slowly, and gaining.

Against the rail, Marble Archer won the war of first place against Lombardy, and the others in the field bunched behind the two of them. Lydia was now somewhere in that crush, but Kate kept losing sight of her. Hal had been right; it was hard to identify each horse continuously.

At the far turn, in fifth place now, Lydia began to gain ground, bearing down on the horses between her and Lombardy. She passed the third- and fourth-position horses, and Kate's heart skipped a beat. "Keep it up," she screamed. "Keep it up." But the pace looked hard for Lydia, and Kate began to worry. At the top of the stretch, Lombardy, in second place, was a couple of lengths ahead of her when, Kate later learned, Tim made his move. Lydia suddenly catapulted forward in an open challenge for his second-place position, running head to head with Lombardy until that big black horse dropped back and let her have it. Kate shouted and banged her program against her hand.

Lydia had just passed him and was beginning to close the ten lengths that lay between her and Marble Archer when Lombardy stumbled, throwing off the frantic pell-mell pace of the horses behind him. A groan arose from the crowd. But the horses seemed to regroup and thundered on as Lombardy lost ground and took fourth position.

The stumble had not affected Lydia, who, with less than a thousand feet to the finish, dug in her toes and surged forward. At that moment, Kate recalled what Hal had always said about her: she wanted to win; she was, indeed, a stayer. Now she was drawing abreast of Marble Archer and the crowd was screaming with one voice. At the seven-eighths pole, she vied with him, stride for stride, nose to nose, as they thundered down in front of the stands. Kate was yelling so loud she could feel the shout in her throat but couldn't hear it in the deafening noise. Once again she saw Lydia call on some reserve of energy from the wonderful machine of her body. She pulled ahead of Marble Archer to finish desperately, triumphantly, by a nose.

"*She's won, she's won,*" Kate heard herself shrieking at the top of her lungs. Hal was reaching for her in what seemed like slow motion; she thought he was fainting. Everyone in the box was jumping up and down in a passionate exultation that they couldn't have controlled if they'd wanted to. Now Kate was in Hal's arms and he was swinging her off the ground, yelling something in her ear. The tears were running down his cheeks. The sounds from the crowd around and below them were like surf—tumultuous, roiling. Kate saw Ann sail her hat into the air; it sailed out over the stands as she clung to Hal's jacket, screaming. From the corner of her eye, Kate could see Lydia cantering down the track, whole and unharmed.

Kate didn't remember how she got to the winner's circle. She kept dabbing at her eyes, clinging to Hal's arm, smiling so widely she thought her cheeks would crack. And then, suddenly, there was Lydia—sweaty, foamy, glistening, breathing hard, supple—in her prime. She had a proud look in her eye; she was high on victory. Someone had wiped her down, for there was very little dirt from the track on her. Photographers clicked scores of pictures and the general clamor, the crowding and pushing, was nearly enough to make Kate physically ill. Lydia wore the huge wreath of derby roses around her neck when Kate next looked at her, and reporters clamored to talk with Hal and Ann, Barney Sheffield and the jockey.

Hal looked wonderfully calm, a huge grin creasing his cheeks and tilting his eyes. He was looking down at Lydia's legs, checking her visually as he stroked her neck lovingly, and put his head against her in an embrace. Then he reached out of the crowd of people around him, grabbed Kate's hand, and pulled her into the circle with him.

"Is my office going to be surprised if they see this photo," Kate yelled in Hal's ear as a dozen photographers snapped shots of them.

"Aren't you glad you decided to stay?" Hal asked softly, his voice hoarse from shouting. His long, dark eyes rested on hers, full of pride and love.

They stood in the receiving barn watching Lydia being sponged down by a groom. All over the barn similar rituals were taking place with the other derby horses. Though the pandemonium had subsided, people were still excited. Knots of owners, trainers, and track officials, grooms, and handlers moved through the barn or stood near their horses, recounting the race.

Outside, photographers and reporters were waiting for interviews, but in here, until Lydia was checked out by the vet, it would remain comparatively calm.

Lydia whinnied softly and rolled her eyes at Hal, but Kate could see she was tired.

"Why—because you're rich?" Kate asked, standing back from him and looking at him with a raised eyebrow.

"Well, not so rich as some people think, and I have to pay taxes on her winnings, but at least I'm solvent." He took her hands. The groom languidly and tenderly sponged Lydia's fine, frail legs. "Marry me, Kate," Hal breathed. She could barely hear him as someone nearby called out to someone else about Lombardy, who had pulled up lame. "Marry me," he repeated in a lull. The groom looked up, smiling.

"Hal," a voice shouted out at the end of the barn; a man in jeans was scuttling toward Hal along the stalls. "Mr. Lewis?" he called.

"Yo," Hal cried.

The man stopped in front of him. "There's a lot of reporters—"

"We'll be right out." Hal turned back to Kate as the man disappeared around the corner of the stall. "Marry me, Kate."

"Funny, I always assumed you were talking about marriage," she said with a lilt in her voice. Kate moved back away from the horse and groom, seeking a little privacy. Hal followed.

"Where are you going?" he asked.

"Isn't there somewhere we can be alone?"

"Here? Today?" He laughed. "No. Stop here. Just tell me what's on your mind." He leaned one shoulder against the wall about thirty feet from Lydia.

"I've done a lot of thinking since last night," she

said quietly, "and I think I've got a compromise to offer you."

"Spoken like a good lawyer." He laughed but his eyes looked worried.

"When you told me how bad things really were last night, I knew I couldn't leave you. You can't love someone the way I love you and walk away when he is in such a deep and risky game." Hal's eyes caressed her face. He was touched but still concerned about what she was going to say.

"What you needed—and still need—is a backer, a partner."

"You."

"Not in that sense. You need a corporation or a partnership with capital. I'm a good partner for you, yes, but I don't want to spend my professional life as your business manager. I will be your adviser, lawyer, friend—lover," she said, lowering her voice. "But I just can't give up my own practice of law. I love the law. No, don't speak yet," she said, putting two fingers on his lips. "This morning I tried to think of ways to help you dig yourself out if Lydia didn't win. Now you don't have that problem but—"

"Hal, where are you?" someone called out.

"In a minute," Hal shouted back. Lydia, hearing his voice, whinnied.

"I want to suggest you consider moving your small, dignified, first-class stables operation with Ann to Southern California." Hal's eyebrows shot up in surprise. "I think I can find investors for you out there."

"Southern California?" Hal asked, not getting the full picture yet.

"Yes. Southern California."

"You mean . . . move there."

"Yes. You and Ann and Lydia. I'll set up the partnership and draw up the papers. I'll handle all the legal work for you—"

Hal couldn't contain himself. "Where's the compromise?"

"*That's* the compromise. You move to Southern California—and so will I. I'll leave San Francisco." She looked up at him, not without trepidation. "I know how much you love Kentucky. You don't have to sell your land now—it can always be here if you want it. If things go well, you'll be racing again in the derby. But I'm asking you to make your working home where I can also practice the kind of law I love in a state whose ways and people I understand. There are firms in Los Angeles that I've had dealings with, and I'm sure I can relocate there. It won't be easy, but it can be done." She took his hand. "Will you marry me?" She felt her chest contract; she'd stopped breathing.

He leaned toward her very slowly and brushed her cheek with his lips. An assistant trainer rushed past them.

"Where do I sign?" he whispered.

"We have a deal?" She grinned.

"We have a deal."

His face was only an inch away from hers, his long, luscious eyes studying hers.

"But you didn't say you'd marry me," she sighed.

"I asked you first, counselor."

"My answer is . . . yes, I'd be proud to," she said. "Proud to."

"Tell me you love me, counselor," he said, his lips touching hers lightly. Someone in back of them whistled, long and low. The sounds of the huge barn were beginning to come back to her—horses stomping and snorting, men calling back and forth, footsteps along wooden planks and hard-packed dirt.

"I love you," she murmured, her lips fluttering against his.

"Tell me you won't ever leave me."

"I won't ever leave you, darling Hal."

His arms reached around her waist and his breath was hot upon her cheeks as his lips pressed hers. She felt her body melding into his as she tasted the sweet tang of his mouth. She raised her arms around him, crushing her lips against his, a cone of delicious happiness spiraling through her. As if from a distance, she heard applause and shouts of approval.

She opened her eyes. A crowd of grooms, owners, and trainers had gathered around them.

"Hal, people are watching," she said, smiling.

"Good. They should know how it's done."

Very slowly and gently they disengaged. Hal waved to the assembly.

"Well, counselor, shall we get on with the partnership?"

TELL US YOUR OPINIONS AND RECEIVE A FREE COPY
OF THE RAPTURE NEWSLETTER.

Thank you for filling out our questionnaire. Your response to the following questions will help us to bring you more and better books. In appreciation of your help we will send you a free copy of the Rapture Newsletter.

1. Book Title:_____

   Book #:_____ (5–7)

2. Using the scale below how would you rate this book on the following features? Please write in one rating from 0–10 for each feature in the spaces provided. Ignore bracketed numbers.

(Poor) 0 1 2 3 4 5 6 7 8 9 10 (Excellent)
                                  0–10 Rating

Overall Opinion of Book................ _____ (8)
Plot/Story.......................... _____ (9)
Setting/Location..................... _____ (10)
Writing Style....................... _____ (11)
Dialogue........................... _____ (12)
Love Scenes........................ _____ (13)
Character Development:
Heroine:........................... _____ (14)
Hero:.............................. _____ (15)
Romantic Scene on Front Cover......... _____ (16)
Back Cover Story Outline .... _____ (17)
First Page Excerpts.................. _____ (18)

3. What is your: Education: Age:_____(20-22)

    High School ( )1   4 Yrs. College (·)3
    2 Yrs. College ( )2   Post Grad   ( )4 (23)

4. Print Name:_____

   Address:_____

   City:_____State:_____Zip:_____

   Phone # ( )_____ (25)

Thank you for your time and effort. Please send to New American Library, Rapture Romance Research Department, 1633 Broadway, New York, NY 10019.

RAPTURE ROMANCE

Provocative and sensual,
passionate and tender—
the magic and mystery of love
in all its many guises

Coming next month

PASSION'S PROMISE by Sharon Wagner. When her long-ago first love Ben Cumberland reentered her life, Joyce Cole felt all her defenses crumbling. But would the passion he promised cost her the independence she'd worked so long to achieve. . . ?

SILK AND STEEL by Kathryn Kent. Though their wills clashed by day, at night Ryan and Laura were joined in sweet ecstasy. But did the successful promoter really love the young fashion designer—or was he only using her talents to settle an old business score?

ELUSIVE PARADISE by Eleanor Frost. For Anne and Jeremy, a private business relationship turned into an emotional, passionate affair—that was soon the focus of a magazine article. Then Anne began to wonder if Jeremy was interested in her, or publicity for their business venture . . .

RED SKY AT NIGHT by Ellie Winslow. Could Nat Langley fulfill trucker Kay O'Hara's every dream? Nat had designed the rig she'd always wanted, and Kay had to find out whether he was trying to sell himself—or his truck—to her . . .

BITTERSWEET TEMPTATION by Jillian Roth. Chase Kincaid haunted Julie King's thoughts long after he'd broken her heart. Now he was back, reawakening dreams and desires, making her fear she'd be hurt again . . .

RECKLESS DESIRE by Nelle Russell. Novelist Justin Reynolds was the most magnetic male Margot Abbott had ever met. But what kind of love story were his caresses creating for Margot, who knew him so little yet wanted him so much. . . ?

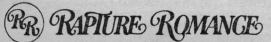

RAPTURE ROMANCE

Provocative and sensual, passionate and tender— the magic and mystery of love in all its many guises
New Titles Available Now

To order, use the convenient coupon on the next page.

RAPTURE ROMANCE

Provocative and sensual, passionate and tender— the magic and mystery of love in all its many guises

---

Buy them at your local bookstore or use coupon on next page for ordering.

RAPTURE ROMANCE

Provocative and sensual, passionate and tender— the magic and mystery of love in all its many guises

---

SPECIAL $1.00 REBATE OFFER
WHEN YOU BUY
FOUR RAPTURE ROMANCES

To receive your cash refund, send:

1. This coupon: To qualify for the $1.00 refund, this coupon, completed with your name and address, must be used. (Certificate may not be reproduced)

2. Proof of purchase: Print, on the reverse side of this coupon, the *title* of the books, the *numbers* of the books (on the upper right hand of the front cover preceding the price), and the U.P.C. numbers (on the back covers) on your next four purchases.

3. Cash register receipts, with prices circled to:
   Rapture Romance $1.00 Refund Offer
   P.O. Box NB037
   El Paso, Texas 79977

Offer good only in the U.S. and Canada. Limit one refund/response per household for any group of four Rapture Romance titles. Void where prohibited, taxed or restricted. Allow 6–8 weeks for delivery. Offer expires March 31, 1984.

NAME_____

ADDRESS_____

CITY_____STATE_____ZIP_____

SPECIAL $1.00 REBATE OFFER
WHEN YOU BUY
FOUR RAPTURE ROMANCES

See complete details on reverse

1. Book Title _____

Book Number 451-_____

U.P.C. Number 7116200195-_____

2. Book Title _____

Book Number 451-_____

U.P.C. Number 7116200195-_____

3. Book Title _____

Book Number 451-_____

U.P.C. Number 7116200195-_____

4. Book Title _____

Book Number 451-_____

U.P.C. Number 7116200195-_____

— U.P.C. Number

0 | SAMPLE |

7 1162 00195